Menzuo

Judgment Set

Upon Earth

Keshawn Dodds

Menzuo

Judgment Set

Upon Earth

Keshawn Dodds

Quality Words Productions™

Publication in Print and Sound on the net

Cosby Media Productions

Entertaining the Mind, and Inspiring the Soul

DEDICATION

This book is dedicated to the Boys & Girls Club Family Center, located in the heart of Springfield, Massachusetts. I hope that one day all of the children that we are serving will become superheroes in their own right. I am a product of this organization, and I am destined to change the thinking of our youth.

Many of the children who have read my books say that I have a wild imagination. I say back to them that it is the spirit of all of you that keeps my mind active.

Jammal a.k.a Menzuo is Keshawn
Solar is Marcus.
We will always be tight.

"Through the eyes of Menzuo and the Solar Warriors, I will save the universe!

TABLE OF CONTENTS

Continued From:

Menzuo:

Legend of the Blue Diamond

"How was your tour?" Solar asked Menzuo as he walked into the room.

"It was cool. I got to see a lot of great things." he said with a smirk as he proudly looked at Solar.

"Well, good, now get some rest. We have a lot to accomplish in the morning," replied Solar in a serious tone.

Menzuo fully understood the gravity of the situation and listened to Solar's request. "Okay, Solar, you get some rest, too," he said as he crawled into the bed.

"My Prince, I have rested long enough. You just regain your energy, and we will be fine."

Without another word, Menzuo sighed and fell asleep. Solar stood by the window and looked out at the life that was constantly

1

regenerating on planet Bralose. He looked up into the dark sky and noticed many shooting stars passing by. It reminded him of the times when he went into battle as the young Warrior, Prince Kenshuo. Solar could remember lighting the skies in the name of peace, as he fought the evil that lived within the universe. Pride filled his soul as the thoughts continued. Solar looked at his hands with pride, happy to be a full person again. His death was avenged with the defeat of Morbid, and now he had a greater purpose. To protect the universe with his younger brother was his only mission, and he didn't want to be anywhere else.

~Menzuo~

Back in her room as Princess Amiata was just about to jump into bed, there was a knock at her door.

"Come in." she said softly.

The door opened slowly. "Hi, honey," King Eojtaf said with a straight face. "I had to come and talk to you before you fell asleep."

Amiata sat on her bed. "Okay, what's up, daddy?"

King Eojtaf took a deep breath and let it out slowly as he sat next to his daughter. He smiled with love as he ran his fingers through her hair. "My beautiful, darling angel, how much I have loved to see you grow. You are the best gift that I have ever received in life."

A tear fell from Princess Amiata's left eye. "Thank you, daddy, I love you too. Don't worry, I promise that I will be careful."

King Eojtaf nodded, then sat back. "Listen, honey," he said strongly. "The road that you are about to travel is very, very dangerous. Nothing that I could have done with you in your short life could have ever prepared you for what you are about to experience. I knew for years that one day, you would be called to do something extraordinary for our universe," he looked at the ceiling. "I knew that this was going to happen the day you were born. You are meant to become a warrior."

"Just like you, daddy?" Amiata questioned.

King Eojtaf shook his head. "No, my dear, even better. As I met Destiera in her room of truth, she told me that one day, I would either make a decision to help save our universe or help to destroy it," he lowered his head. "Now I truly understand what she meant by that," King Eojtaf picked up his head and looked deep into his daughter's eyes. "I see that the decision wasn't for me to succeed in any battle, rather it is for me to let my daughter fight by Prince Menzuo's side, so that is what I am going to do. I will do anything to help save our universe, even if it means having my darling girl, do it in my place. I am not the one to stand in the way of destiny, even if it means breaking the laws that I have put forth, for the royal family."

A smile fell across Amiata's face. "I am so happy to have a father like you," she gave him a big hug. "I have always looked up to you. I want to be just as good of a warrior as you once were. I want to make the people of our planet proud of me."

As she let go, King Eojtaf smiled. "They already are, my dear. You do not have to prove anything to us. You only have to fulfill your destiny now. Never worry about what we think. You have proven yourself worthy by having our planet saved. At the same time, your mother and I were captured, and our people were under Hydrosion's control."

Amiata lowered her head. "Thank you, father," she said as King Eojtaf lifted her head gently by the chin. He kissed her on the cheek then hugged her tight. He held his daughter as tightly, knowing that hug may be the last one that he would receive for a long time.

As King Eojtaf pulled away, he wiped the tears from her face. "Now, since you are going to journey into the realm of warriors, I must give you this to help you on your way," he reached into his pocket.

"What is it, father?" asked Amiata curiously.

King Eojtaf slowly pulled a silver bracelet from his pocket. "This is the Bralokian warrior's manacle. This manacle will give you extra energy to fight in battle. Once you place it on, you will be recognized as a true Bralokian Warrior," he slowly held it in front of Amiata's face.

She held out her hand, waiting for her father to drop it. "Thank you. I will not let you down."

King Eojtaf smiled. "I know you will do your best to honor the Bralokian way. I can sense the fight flowing through your body. You will not let us down. Like I said, no matter what you do, as long as you are fighting in our honor, you will always make us proud," he dropped the manacle into the palm of her hand.

Amiata grabbed it as tightly as she could then looked back into her father's eyes. "Thank you so much, daddy. I truly love you for letting me pursue my dreams," she gave him a kiss on the cheek. As she did, the door to her room opened. Princess Amiata noticed the light coming in. "Hi, mommy," she said happily. She let go of her father slowly.

"Hello, honey," she responded. Queen Vanera noticed the bracelet in her hand. "Well, I see that you have received your father's manacle. I know that you will wear it proudly."

"Yes, I will, mother. I am ready to fight for Bralose's honor."

Queen Vanera shook her head with a smile. "I often wonder what has happened to my sweet, little girl."

Amiata stood up and walked over to her mother. "She has grown up, but no matter what I do, mommy, I will always be your little girl."

Queen Vanera hugged her tightly. "Thank you for that, honey. I love you."

"I love you too, mommy."

King Eojtaf stood and walked over to his two girls. "Well, my Queen, I believe that our moment has come and gone. Our girl is no longer, little," he kissed Amiata on her forehead and grabbed his wife's hand. "Make us proud, honey."

Amiata bowed to both of her parents. They respectfully bowed as well. Queen Vanera sighed heavily. "Get some rest, honey. You have a critical day ahead of you," she said.

"Okay, mother," Amiata responded as her parents backed out of the room.

They all smiled at each other as the door slowly closed. "Goodbye, honey," King Eojtaf said softly.

"Goodnight," Amiata said back. The door closed, leaving Amiata standing alone in her room. She took a deep breath then looked at what was still in her hand. "The Bralokian Warrior's, manacle. I've always wanted one of these, and now I have my own," she carefully slipped it onto her wrist. She watched it adjust comfortably to her size. As it did, a surge of energy flowed through her body. Her eyes quickly lit up. "Whoa!" she said happily. Now, as a true Bralokian Warrior, Princess Amiata was ready for battle.

~Menzuo~

Menzuo slept comfortably in his bed in the castle, and with Solar bringing him to his peaceful resting place, the young Prince's body was able to relax.

Without warning, Menzuo's peaceful dream was invaded by the sounds of an unknown battle. Flashes of terrorized faces and broken screams interrupted the soft sounds of water crashing below into the river. "Help...help!" someone continued to scream.

Menzuo rolled over in his bed as the flashes of exploding buildings and visions of hundreds of people running away from falling objects slipped into his dream.

The images stopped as Menzuo was transferred from the grassy knoll, right to his training area. As he was thrust into the chair, he tried his best to figure out what he was looking at. The young Prince sat back and watched the complete destruction of a city. He continued to hear all of the people screaming loudly as everything blew up around them.

"Aaah, help us! Somebody, please help us!" the people in this unknown burning city continued to scream as they ran for safety. Fire and smoke filled the entire area.

"This isn't right at all," Menzuo shouted as he clenched the arms of the chair. He continued to watch several people run for safety.

Solar noticed, Menzuo struggling in the bed and could sense that he was experiencing danger. He closed his eyes and made himself into his spirit light and entered the blue diamond.

Right as he did, he could see Menzuo sitting in his training area. He rushed to his side. As he floated next to his brother, he made his self-whole again. They were now seeing everything together.

"What is this?" Solar asked.

"I don't know," Menzuo responded. I was taken from my resting place and brought here. All of this is crazy. Where is this, and is this Lord Fetid's doing?"

Solar shook his head as the view floated over several burning buildings. "No, I don't believe so. This place looks very familiar, though, and what I am sensing is an unknown evil." Solar paused as the view shot over the skyline of the city. It quickly hit him. "Oh, no!"

Menzuo looked to his brother. "What is it, Solar?"

"This…this is, Hero City. There is an evil that has been awakened."

"What evil?"

Before Menzuo could respond, a voice shouted out to him. "Menzuo!" the screenshot through the streets of the city then stopped right in front of a person. The smoke-blackened his body, but Menzuo and Solar noticed the silhouette of this person as he continued. "I know that you can hear me, and I can also hear you. There is a growing evil here in Hero City."

Menzuo looked at the silhouette very confused. "Who are you, and how are you talking to me? What is happening there?"

"I do not have much time to explain, but my name is Paladin, and I am the last living guardian of Hero City. The awakened dark spores have been released. For many years, this dark energy has been dormant on our planet. I have done all that I can to keep it locked and sealed away. Due to a combination of events that have taken place on our planet. Your battles and the battles with several other heroes, the dark spores have risen."

"How have they been awakened, and what is a dark spore?"

"These Dark Spores are evil that can destroy all of humanity. One of Excervo's Pirate Drones was able to infiltrate the sealed fortress where they were being held. This thing mixed its dark blood with the spores and gave it an uncontrollable amount of power. I have the Drone in my custody, but the damage has been done. The dark spores have been released, and you can see the carnage that they are causing all around Hero City."

"A Pirate Drone, that thing is from…"

"Planet Excervo, I know," Paladin said, cutting Menzuo off. "I know all about you and your life's mission, but there is no time for me to go into details on how I know all of this. What I need from you is to get here as soon as possible, but you must handle a threat that can possibly overtake our world. There is a serious threat that is attacking us from all angles. Springfield is currently under attack by a Pirate Queen known as Eaziah. There are several other known heroes that I am contacting, and they must survive for us to bring peace back to our planet. They are enduring similar battles on their home fronts. Menzuo, you are critical to the success of our world."

"Solar, this is strange. How does he know all of this about me, and how is there another Pirate released this quickly? This goes against everything that I have learned about Excervo," Menzuo whispered.

"I'm not sure. First off, I have no knowledge of this man, but his energy is pure, I can sense it. Also, everything that we have learned about Excervo has changed. We will have to get more answers as to how Lord Fetid released another Pirate."

Menzuo directed his attention back to the silhouette. "Okay, Paladin, I will be there as soon as I can. How can I find you?"

A loud explosion occurred right behind the silhouette of Paladin, almost knocking him off of his feet. "Just show up, I will find you!"

Another loud explosion went off just as a monster ran into the mist, charging towards Paladin. Without hesitation, the hero destroyed the beast, then stepped forward. "Take care of your duties and protect our world like the warrior that I know you are."

Several screams filled the room as one last explosion went off. The silhouette of Paladin disappeared, and the place went black.

"He's gone!" Menzuo said as he fell back into the chair. He clenched his teeth as hard as he could.

"Help! Help us!" someone yelled.

Menzuo directed his attention to his left. The training room went utterly black then slowly came into focus again. Menzuo sat back and watched the complete destruction of his home city of Springfield. He could hear all of the people screaming loudly as everything blew up around them.

"Paladin was right," Menzuo stated, "there is a serious threat attacking my home."

People within the city continued to scream as they ran for safety. Hundreds of military planes and helicopters flew in from every direction, teamed up to battle the evil that found its way onto the planet. They were circling the sky, shooting bullets and missiles at an object.

Menzuo couldn't clearly see what it was that continued to hover just below the clouds. He knew that it had to be the Pirate Queen Eaziah. Menzuo desperately wanted to see her face. Thousands of explosions from the military's attacks shook in Menzuo.

Fighter planes attacked from the sky, while submarines assaulted from below. This war was taking place with millions of silky black and yellow aliens. Their sharp teeth and claws were invading the ground, growling and maliciously blowing up everything that was in front of them.

Cars were blasted into the sky as these aliens chased and captured every person who was in their sight. When they did get their hands on someone, a cloud of smoke filled the area. The alien, along with the human, disappeared instantly into thin air.

"This isn't right at all," Menzuo shouted as he clenched the arms of the chair. The people were transported out of the planet, and out to planet Excervo. They were set to become Lord Fetid's slaves.

Queen Eaziah could destroy everything all over the city without fear of the military attacks against her. Buildings and houses were crumbling by the second. Springfield was becoming the most violent battle zone ever seen within the universe, and no one was able to put a stop to it.

A few seconds later, Menzuo and Solar heard someone scream. "Menzuo! Solar Please help!"

Menzuo shot up out of the seat as he and Solar focused on the screams. The vision was quickly transferred through the burning city directly to Menzuo's home.

"Help ... please help!" the voice screamed again.

Solar focused harder on the voice and found his dog Barkley hiding in a hidden room. It was dimly lit, but he could see his friend and several people lying on the ground behind him.

A few seconds later, Solar could see him as well. "Barkley, where are you?

He looked around, perplexed, "Something is wrong. All of these terrible monsters are destroying our city. They are being led by some lady floating in the sky. Her energy was so strong and scary."

Menzuo and Solar looked on worriedly as they continued to hear explosions and other people's screams from the outside of where his dog was. "Are you okay, and where are my parents?" Menzuo asked.

"I am fine. Everyone has passed out from the smoke. They are safe for now. I found a hidden room in the basement of the house and led everyone down here. Allucio and Desmurose's parents are here as well," Barkley said as he continued to breathe slowly. "Those monsters are taking everyone from here."

Menzuo balled his fists tightly as he stood up next to Solar. "Did you hear anything from that floating lady in the sky?" Solar asked.

"Yes, she was calling out for you, Menzuo. It was bizarre. She kept appearing all over the city, releasing those ugly beasts, letting them fall from the sky. I could hear her clearly from inside of the house," a massive cloud of smoke covered her face," Barkley paused for a minute to cough. It was getting hard for him to breathe as he continued. "Everyone was sitting in the kitchen when your dad noticed something flash on the television. He turned the volume up, and there she was on the news."

"Did you see where she was last?" Menzuo asked.

"Yes, she was floating above our house. That was the last time that I saw her. She knows that you are from here. She's close, I can still feel her presence."

Menzuo started to breathe slowly. "My parents! My friends! All of those people on the planet!" he yelled as the explosions grew louder.

Solar stood confidently in the room. "Try to keep yourself safe, Barkley. We're coming soon."

Just as Solar said that another loud explosion shook the room that Barkley and his parents were in. "Hurry!" he shouted.

The picture on him faded quickly as his voice echoed in the room.

Menzuo jumped. "Barkley!"

"He's gone!" Menzuo said as he sank into the chair. Menzuo clenched his teeth as hard as he could.

"It's time to leave, my Prince. Wake up!" replied Solar in a stern tone.

In an instant, Menzuo popped up in a cold sweat. He looked over to Solar as he continued to breathe slowly. The sun was coming up over planet Bralose and shining directly onto Solar's face.

A tear slowly ran down Menzuo's cheek. "Those beasts are going to pay for what they have done."

Solar nodded in agreement. "Yes, they will, my Prince. Get yourself ready, I'll round everyone up. Meet us out front."

Menzuo nodded. He made his power suit return then walked over to the window. He looked up into the sky as he wiped a tear from his face. "I'll be home soon, everyone. Just hang in there," he closed his eyes, letting the visions of horror flow through his mind once again. He took one last deep breath before opening his revenge filled eyes. Menzuo nodded. "Now, I am ready," he walked out of the room and down the hallway.

As Menzuo continued on with Solar by his side, he heard voices coming from the dining room. He paused in front of the door and opened it slowly. He noticed that everyone was already in there, ready to journey back to Earth. "We're ready when you are, Prince Menzuo," Princess Amiata said. She was draped in a red and black Bralokian warrior's suit.

This was new to Menzuo, and it was the first official revealing of Princess Amiata's true warrior's side. "Whoa! You really are a warrior!"

Princess Amiata nodded. "Yes, but when Hydrosion attacked my planet, I couldn't use my powers because he held my parents captive. Because of you, I am now able to stand strong in my true form."

Nuncio broke a smile. "My Princess is the King of the Warrior's Gauntlet. She is ready for battle."

Allucio scratched his head. "King of the Warrior's Gauntlet? But you're a girl?"

Princess Amiata chuckled. "It's a long story that I can tell you while we travel to Earth."

"I'm always down for a good story," Desmurose interjected, keeping the feelings light in the room."

Menzuo nodded with a stone look on his face. He could feel the urgency and confidence coming from each of his friends. They all were ready to battle for Earth's safety. "Okay, then. Nuncio, please bring us to the ship; we're ready to go," Menzuo said. He turned and walked out of the dining room without saying another word.

Everyone quickly followed. They walked towards the front doors of the castle, straight to the spaceship. The young warriors knew that this mission may be their last.

As they all boarded the ship, Princess Amiata looked back and noticed her mother and father standing on the balcony. They looked at each other lovingly for a minute. King Eojtaf blew his little girl a kiss to wish her much safety as she left on her journey with the rest of the warrior's. Amiata reached into the air and acted as if she was able to catch the kiss. She then put her hand onto her heart then bowed. She turned and slowly walked onto the ship.

"That's our daughter. Amiata has set out on her life's destiny. How very proud I am of her today," King Eojtaf said with a smile running across his face.

Queen Vanera gently grabbed him by the waist and pulled her husband closer. "She will be just fine, Eojtaf. She has some wonderful people around her and not to mention, Nuncio. He will never let anything happen to our daughter."

King Eojtaf nodded as he watched the ship float into the sky. He could see Amiata looking out of the window directly at him. A few seconds later, the aircraft shot off like a missile. Through the clouds and quickly from the planet, the Solar Warriors were on their way to Earth.

"Be safe, all of you. My heart and soul shall comfort you, young warriors, in your times of need. Thank you once again for saving planet Bralose," King Eojtaf said as the wind blew gently through his planet.

Chapter 1

Master Renzfly's Urgent Message

There was a strange quietness on the ship as they flew out of planet Bralose and towards the inner realm. As they flew past planet Walonoke, Scoop made his way over to Menzuo and sat down next to him. "You know, Menzuo," he said, finally breaking the long silence, "it takes a lot of courage to do what you have just done."

Menzuo looked at him, somewhat confused. "What do you mean, Scoop?"

Scoop leaned forward in his chair. Everyone was listening in on their conversation. "You have just saved a planet from near extinction from a deadly Pirate Warrior, and you wouldn't stop until you got the job done. Also, to go in and face a mythical creature, like the Naleezar, was unbelievable. I have to admit, after spending many years under that monster's control, I didn't give you an ounce of hope. I just knew that you were going to be that 'thing's' next meal, but you proved me wrong. I could have passed out and died right then and there when I saw you fly out of that saliva waterfall with the blue diamond. The way that you flew through the Onyx Forest, towards the exit…wow! That was utterly amazing," Scoop leaned over to the window, looking out to his home planet. "You know what? I wonder what that Naleezar is thinking right now."

A smile finally fell upon Menzuo's face as Scoop sat back in his chair. "He's probably trying to figure out how to cover up the hole that I left in his head after I stole his eye."

"Ha, ha, ha, I know. I'm still trying to figure out how you took it," the smile slowly left Scoops face and was replaced with a very disgusted look. "Well, maybe I don't want to know. I'm just happy that I'm free. Thank you, Menzuo, for saving me."

Menzuo looked over to him. "No problem, Scoop, but just imagine if I didn't save you. I probably wouldn't know what to do with this blue diamond, and life as we know it might have ended. You are a major part of that success, you know?"

"Cough…cough…cough…ahem!" Wyler leaned forward, grabbing Menzuo's attention.

Menzuo chuckled. "You too, Wyler, I couldn't have done any of this without you as well."

Everyone smiled and felt a little more at ease for the time being, as they flew closer to the vortex.

As Nuncio continued to fly the ship.

Solar watched the stars pass from out of the window that he sat next to. At that moment, he felt an immense energy shoot through his body. "WHOA! What was that?" he said as he jumped to his feet.

Everyone's smile quickly left their faces as they focused their attention on him. "What is it, Solar?" Menzuo said as he sat up.

"I don't know, but whatever it is, it's powerful," Solar responded as he balled his fists.

"What should I do, Solar? I can't feel that energy, but I am concerned," Nuncio said frantically.

"Just keep flying. I can't tell whether the power is good or evil," Solar explained.

"Whatever it is, we'll be ready for it," Scoop answered with confidence.

Everyone started to breathe slowly as they looked out of the windows of the ship.

"Whoa! I felt it! How can something be that strong?" Menzuo shouted

"Whoa!" Desmurose yelled out as the surge went through him.

"Whoa!" Amiata followed. "This is unreal!"

One after another, they felt an intense energy, getting closer. "Stay focused, everyone. This might be the beginning of the battle. Queen Eaziah may know of our location," Solar said in a stern tone, keeping everyone alert.

Nuncio looked out of the window and noticed a planet nearby. "I'll land on planet Pryzor," he shouted. "We'll have a better chance to fight there than in space."

"Okay, but hurry! It's getting closer. Be careful while flying into that planet, we do not need an explosion hitting this ship," Solar said as he focused on the stars out north.

With an abrupt turn, Nuncio quickly headed for Pryzor.

A few moments later, they entered the planet's atmosphere. Nuncio maneuvered the ship through a bunch of floating objects that had very pointy spikes hanging from them. As he continued, each peak was just inches from hitting them.

Nuncio descended towards the ground. With swift, precise movements, he successfully steered the ship through the unknown threats. He safely landed in the middle of a blue desert.

The doors to the ship opened, and everyone quickly exited, looking up at the sky. "What are those things over our heads?" Menzuo asked curiously. They all looked at the objects floating about fifty feet above them.

"These are floating cacti, gas bubbles," Solar answered. "This planet is volatile and can easily blow up if too many of these cacti explode. Plus, the gas inside of them is very poisonous."

"Then why did we land here?" Allucio asked. "The Queen could now easily take us out if she wanted."

Nuncio shook his head. "She wouldn't blow this planet up."

"Why? I thought Pirates didn't care about life," Desmurose said curiously.

"They do not care about life, but they care about what this planet produces," Nuncio answered as he continued to look up. "This cacti gas is essential to the structure of the universe. This gas is filtered to the existing planets for energy in the outer realm, even Excervo. They know how important this planet is to our system. That is why Pryzor will never suffer a heavy attack from any evil."

"So, we are safe from any type of battle here?" Menzuo asked quickly.

"As long as we are here, yes," Nuncio responded. "This is the universes neutral planet."

"Wait!" Solar shouted, grabbing everyone's attention. "The energy is getting stronger!" his heart was beating faster.

A flash of light-filled a space in Pryzor's sky. "Here it comes!" Wyler yelled. "Everyone, get ready!"

They all quickly powered up.

As Solar got ready to enter the blue diamond, Menzuo shouted. "Wait! Solar, I know who it is."

Solar made himself whole again as he focused on the energy. He looked into the sky with a smile. The white light was growing more significant as it closed in on them. "I wonder why he is coming."

Everyone looked at the both of them very confused. They all started to relax as they noticed the lack of urgency in Solar and Menzuo.

"Who is it? Who is coming?" Allucio asked.

Menzuo smiled as the light quickly faded behind the floating gas cacti. As it did, another ship broke through Pryzor's atmosphere. "It's my trainer, Master Renzfly."

The aircraft slowly floated towards the ground as everyone's energy level went back to normal. The Solar Warriors waited patiently for Master Renzfly to exit. As the ship's engine finally rested, the doors slowly opened, and Master Renzfly appeared.

"Wow, he's ripped!" Desmurose shouted excitedly.

"He's on our side?" Allucio asked with his eyes wide.

Menzuo nodded. "Yes, he is."

Menzuo and Solar walked over, confidently. As they did, a smile fell upon Master Renzfly's face. "This is a pleasant surprise," he said as he looked at Menzuo's new power suit. "I see that you have found the blue diamond and inherited some Walonokian magic."

Menzuo looked down at the blue diamond and at his new suit. He nodded. "Yeah, and it wasn't easy getting all of this."

Master Renzfly agreed. "Nothing ever is, my Prince," he looked over to Solar. Master Renzfly took in a deep breath and let it out slowly. "I see that the body of Prince Kenshuo has returned to you. This is also a wonderful surprise."

Solar held his hands out and looked at them. "Yes, I guess so, but Menzuo and I are still linked together. I still have to be inside of the blue diamond whenever we battle. I do not have enough energy to fight outside of it yet, but that is just fine with me. I'm just happy that I can now live outside of the blue diamond and see the universe with my own eyes."

Master Renzfly nodded and looked to the others. He walked over with a straight face. "So, this is how you two have turned out, Allucio and Desmurose, I knew that I chose two great kids to be by Prince Menzuo's side."

They both looked at each other in confusion, then back at Master Renzfly. "I'm sorry, but how do you know us?" Allucio asked.

"I was the one who chose your families to go to planet Earth. I wanted two young men to be by Menzuo's side at all times. When you two were born, I knew that the three of you would make great friends."

Desmurose shook his head. "Man and I thought that I knew everything about our past."

Master Renzfly shook his head, with a slight chuckle. He then walked over to the Princess and bowed. "Greetings, Princess Amiata, it is a pleasure to meet the daughter of a great Bralokian Warrior."

"It is nice to finally meet you too, Master Renzfly. I have heard many great things about you as well."

He lifted his head. "To you, Nuncio, it is nice to see you again. I know the King wouldn't let his daughter go on this journey without you by her side. Menzuo and the others are lucky to have you around as well."

"Thank you, Master Renzfly, for the compliment," Nuncio said respectfully.

Master Renzfly made his way over to Scoop and Wyler. "Wyler, my friend, it's nice to see that you have joined Menzuo out of his training realm," he turned to Scoop, "but I am not sure that I have met you."

Wyler stepped forward. "This is the former King of planet Walonoke, King Scoop, the one that I told you about. I was linked with him to protect the planet before I was assigned to be with

Menzuo. Prince Menzuo saved him from the Naleezar, and we were once again reunited."

Master Renzfly nodded. "I see. Well, it's a pleasure to meet you, King Scoop, and thank you for coming."

"I am honored to meet you, Master Renzfly," Scoop responded. "The Walonokian tribe firmly stands by the people who help to protect us. It is only right for me to journey with Prince Menzuo after what he has done for my people and me."

After the introductions, Menzuo spoke. "So, why are you here?"

Master Renzfly took in an intense breath. His smile quickly changed back to the serious expression that he usually had. "You all must come with me. Follow my ship to planet Yardania. You cannot go back to Earth at this moment."

"But why not," Desmurose shouted quickly as Master Renzfly walked back to his ship. "What about our parents, our friends, and all of those people?"

Menzuo promptly shook his head. "Don't question him. He won't answer you. Just get in the ship. We'll find out why in a minute."

Desmurose turned his face up and followed everyone without saying another word. "I just wanted to know what's going on, geez! Is that a crime?" he said sarcastically.

They all entered their ships and quickly shot out of planet Pryzor, away from the inner realm, back towards Yardania.

~Menzuo~

As they continued to fly, they blew past Bralose and noticed that the planet was clearing of its brown, poisonous cloud. They could see the land had fully replenished itself.

"Wow, I can't believe how good my home looks," Amiata said as they passed. She let out a sigh of relief. Although she was ready for what was ahead of her, everyone could tell that she already missed being home.

A few minutes later, they were just a couple of miles from Yardania. Master Renzfly's voice came in over their intercom. "Okay, you all must stay very close to my ship. We will be entering Yardania's atmosphere, pretty quickly. There is a strong force field around the planet. It will only be down for a few seconds, so Nuncio, do your best to stay directly behind me. If you slow up, you will not make it."

"Okay, Master Renzfly," Nuncio responded. He sped up and flew directly behind his ship. "I'm on your tail. We're ready to enter."

"Good. Here we go!" Renzfly said.

Everyone sat back in their seats as Nuncio flew the ship with confidence. Solar sat next to him in the co-pilot's seat. "Hang on, everyone! This may get a little rough," he yelled.

27

The ships quickly closed in on Yardania. They all noticed the blue force field being lowered through their windows. "It's down!" Nuncio shouted. He got as close as he could to Master Renzfly's ship as they broke through the planet's atmosphere.

The ship shook violently. The vibrations made it feel as if the plane was going to be ripped apart. "We're almost there!" Solar yelled as the blue force field lit up the sky once again.

Both ships continued to shake violently as Nuncio regained its balance. "Got it, we're in!" he shouted with excitement.

Just as he gained full control, the spaceship stopped shaking. They slowly broke through the clouds, noticing the beautiful planet of Yardania, below. "Good job, Nuncio," Master Renzfly said encouragingly. "You are a great pilot."

"Thank you, Master Renzfly. You're not too bad yourself," Nuncio responded with relief.

Everyone slowly got out of their seats and walked over to the windows to look. "So, this is our home planet?" Desmurose asked.

Solar walked to the back. "Yes, this is. Welcome home."

Allucio and Desmurose looked at Menzuo with smiles. They were somewhat happy to have finally returned to their birthplace. They all looked out of the window again. Menzuo noticed a massive valley with a bright blue waterfall out of his window. "Solar, why does this place look so familiar?"

"This is where I bring you when you require a true rest. This is one of the most relaxing places in the entire universe."

"I can see why," Amiata added as she watched the water hit the rocks then roll down to the mouth of the river. "I wish that I could come here, as well. It seems like this place could ease your mind from all of the problems that you have to deal with."

Menzuo looked at her with a calming smile. "It really does. I'll make sure that we all make a trip back here after we deal with Queen Eaziah."

Everyone looked at Menzuo then nodded, letting him know that they were behind him.

"Look, we're about to land," Nuncio pointed out, grabbing their attention. "There is the castle just ahead."

"Everybody, get ready," Master Renzfly said over the intercom. We are about to enter the royal grounds."

Menzuo looked at Solar. "Is this where our family lives?"

Solar nodded. "Yes, it is, but I don't think we are here for a family reunion," Solar stood in front of his brother. "I think that it would be best if I stay inside of the blue diamond while we are here. I do not want to startle anyone with my presence."

Menzuo nodded. "I understand."

Both ships landed right at the bottom of the steps to the castle. They all quickly exited the vessels and followed Master Renzfly up to the castle doors.

As they reached the top of the steps, they noticed two elite, Yardanian Warriors, guarding the entrance.

"Hey, they're wearing the same type of fighting gear as Master Renzfly," Allucio whispered to the group.

They all stopped in front of the door. "Greetings, Master Renzfly. King Zenshuo is waiting for you in the royal meeting room."

The two guards opened the huge golden doors. Everyone walked in confidently.

No one said a word as they continued to walk down the long hallway.

Menzuo noticed many pictures of his family hanging on the wall. There were pictures, showing generations of Yardanian royalty and also, of the many elite warriors, trained to protect the planet. Everyone looked around in awe as they studied each picture. They were lost in the moment. The warrior's on the walls were some of the most potent fighter's that ever protected the universe. Although they were gone, their legacy would never be forgotten.

"Wow! These guys look strong!" Allucio whispered as they walked closer to the end of the hallway.

"Maybe we will all have the honor to will placed up there one day," Desmurose said with confidence.

A few seconds later, they all stopped and stood in front of two solid green doors. "We're here," Master Renzfly said, in a severe tone. "Behind these doors, you will see and hear some alarming news. Whatever is said in the royal conference room, you will deal with it. Do not question the universal panel's decisions," he looked directly at Menzuo. "Is that understood?"

They all nodded. Master Renzfly turned and opened the doors. They walked in, ready to hear the concerns of the universal panel.

Chapter 2
Judgment Set Upon Earth

The Solar Warrior's walked into the dimly lit room with many different people sitting in the oval arena.

"So, this is the royal conference room?" Menzuo asked.

"Yes, and these are all of the royal Kings, Queens, and Ambassadors of each planet. They are sitting in their rightful places. They make all of the decisions for our universe's survival," Master Renzfly explained.

Menzuo looked around and noticed Kings and Queens from every planet. The seats that planet Bralose occupied was empty. His eyes made their way to the positions where Earth's representatives were supposed to be. Menzuo noticed that Ambassador Naos was sitting there by himself with a somber and disgusted look on his face. "Where's mother, Earth, Anisa?"

Master Renzfly didn't answer as King Zenshuo slammed down his gavel, quieting the crowd. "All rise," he shouted. Everyone stood as he continued. "I now call to order the judgment set upon Earth. Please be seated and view the findings on our universal screen."

All of the Kings, Queens, and Ambassadors sat quietly and looked to the center of the room. At that moment, the lights went out. A floating screen appeared in front of the Solar Warriors. They all took a few steps back and looked at it curiously. The picture on the screen was covered in a pink fog.

"What is this?" Allucio whispered.

"Keep your eyes on the screen," Master Renzfly whispered back.

As they concentrated, the warriors noticed that the pink cloud started to fade. As it did, a picture of Earth came through, from high in the sky.

"It's our home," Desmurose said quickly to Menzuo and Allucio.

The young warriors were frozen on the royal conference room floor. Menzuo's eyes were glued to the screen as the picture shifted towards the land below. In that instant, they all noticed massive explosions, with fire and smoke, filling the city. It was so loud that the entire universal panel jumped back in shock. Buildings, cars, and houses were blowing up, right before their eyes. Continued excitement filled the room. Mumbles from the royalty expressed great concern for the survival of the planet.

As they continued to watch the mayhem on the floating screen unfold, they all noticed a scary, black and yellow figure running past the screen, growling loudly. As the beast did, they heard people screaming for help.

"What's going on?" Allucio yelled.

Before anyone could answer, the picture floated higher into the sky, showing a top view of the disaster below.

Master Renzfly leaned over to him. "Those are the Pirate Drones, from planet Excervo. They're helping Queen Eaziah take over your city. Their mayhem if not controlled will spread throughout the world."

Menzuo looked on with disgust as he once again watched the swarm of Pirate Drones, invading his home town. "This is sickening!" he snarled as the screen floated back towards the ground. "How could they get away with this?"

"Aah, help! Please…no!" a single human screamed frantically, as a bunch of Pirate Drones chased him. He continued to yell for help as one of the Drones quickly picked him up. Just as it grabbed hold of him, a cloud of black smoke filled the area, and they both disappeared.

Everyone in the room gasped at the sight of this human disappearing right before their eyes.

"What? Where did they go?" Scoop said curiously.

"They're kidnapping the humans. This is not good at all!" Nuncio responded.

People from all over the city were being sucked into the black smoke and taken from Earth. "What are they going to do with them?" Allucio said as his heart started to beat faster.

"They're going to make them slaves on planet Excervo. The humans will live there until the Pirates have no use for them," Master Renzfly responded with a blank look on his face.

"We have to get them back," Menzuo said urgently. "I can't let all of those people suffer like that."

Just as Menzuo finished speaking, the picture flew back into the sky and focused on a floating figure.

"Is that, Queen Eaziah?" Desmurose asked.

The woman had long, silky blue hair that draped over her right shoulder. It fell gently down to her waist. She was wrapped in a long, deep red dress that hugged tightly to her body.

"Yes, that is her," Master Renzfly growled.

"Whoa! She's kinda' beautiful…for an evil Pirate, I mean," Allucio said as he shrugged his shoulders.

"Just wait until she gets angry. She's a whole different beast then," Master Renzfly responded.

Queen Eaziah floated higher in the sky, above the carnage, and watched with a smile. It was as if she was feeding off of the destruction. She floated around the city and listened to every human, cry for help, as they were being plucked from Earth and brought to Excervo.

The universal screen drifted closer to her face as she started to speak. "Soon, this planet will be free of all these worthless humans, and I can search for the energy of all good and evil, without anything getting in my way. Nothing will stop me. Nothing will ever stop me!" Eaziah shouted then took a deep breath as she stroked her silky blue hair. "Mmm, what a beautiful ending to this meaningless planet, and welcome to a great beginning to the reign of Lord Fetid."

Just as she finished speaking, hundreds of fighter planes and helicopters flew in from every direction, surrounding her in the sky. "This is Captain Johnson, of the United States, Air Force. Give yourself up, or we will be forced to open fire!" he barked.

Master Renzfly shook his head. "Bad move. The human army doesn't even stand a fighting chance."

"I'm warning you again! Give yourself up, or we'll have to open fire!" Captain Johnson shouted again.

Queen Eaziah looked around at the fighter planes and helicopters, with a smile. She blew a kiss at the captain. "Oh, how sweet you all are. Willing to die to save your planet. I know that you must try, so, be my guest, open fire. Give me all that you've got, my little babies. You won't be sorry about the outcome. I promise you."

The Captain looked to the other pilots then nodded. "FIRE!" he screamed.

All of the fighter pilots quickly followed his command and unleashed a furious attack. Hundreds of rounds of bullets and missiles flew towards the Queen. Each pilot emptied every bit of ammunition that they had in their arsenal.

Within seconds, the sky was filled with fire and a huge black cloud of smoke. The cloud hovered in the place where Queen Eaziah was. "Hold your fire! Hold your fire!" Captain Johnson shouted to his troops.

After a few moments, the cloud of smoke slowly faded. All of the pilots waited patiently. They were hoping that Queen Eaziah had been destroyed.

"Mmm, that felt wonderful," Queen Eaziah said softly as the smoke finally cleared. She was still floating in the same spot, without a scratch on her body. She pointed to her stomach. "I think you all missed a spot."

The captain pulled off his headset. His eyes widened in disbelief. He couldn't blink as he looked at the Queen. He slowly put his helmet back on and screamed. "Retreat…retreat!"

All of the fighter pilots turned in the opposite direction and started to fly away. Queen Eaziah shook her head, "Tisk, tisk, tisk.

You all came out to play with me then leave before I get a chance to have any fun. What a lousy way to treat a lady," she sighed heavily as the planes were making their way out of the area. "I guess I have to show you all how it's done," she lowered her head. As she did, the wind quickly picked up, making her hair blow violently. Queen Eaziah's, silky blue hair, started to form into two enormous, sharp horns. Her face stretched as her mouth widened. Her sharp teeth were quickly growing and hanging from the sides of her lips.

"Okay, that was a waste of a beautiful face," Allucio said immediately.

Just as he spoke, Queen Eaziah raised her hand and stopped every pilot from flying any farther away. "Please, don't run, my lovelies. I just want to give you all a little kiss."

Captain Johnson looked around at all of the planes and helicopters as they were suspended in mid-air. "Eject...eject!" he screamed.

As the helpless pilots', parachutes opened, Queen Eaziah kissed her hand. She blew it towards the planes and helicopters that floated, motionless in the sky. Captain Johnson and the other pilots descended, looking up. They watched their aircrafts being crushed like soda cans, right before their eyes.

Queen Eaziah ran her tongue across her sharp teeth. "I just wanted to show you a little love, that's all!" she said in a sinister tone. Her laughter echoed through the sky.

Menzuo looked on, angrier than ever. "She has no care for life, does she?"

"Not one single ounce of her soul will ever show any care for life. Pirate Warriors are not designed to care, they are built for destruction and takeover," Master Renzfly replied. He could see the rage building in Prince Menzuo's eyes. "That's why she is the most dangerous Pirate Warrior of them all. Lord Fetid knows that you are capable of handling his other Pirate Warriors in their current state of strength. By sending his wife, he is sending a message to end this war before it even gets started. This could get very ugly."

"Uglier than what I'm looking at right now?" Desmurose said with his eyes as wide as they could get. He shook his head and sighed heavily, "Oh, boy."

"Ha, ha, ha, ha!" the Queens sinister laughter echoed throughout the city. The fighter pilots, floated closer to the ground, towards the waiting Pirate Drones.

The Drones didn't waste any time to capture them. As they were just a few feet away from the ground, the pilots were covered in black smoke, and just like every other helpless human, they disappeared without a trace.

Queen Eaziah held her hands out, expressing the joy of her planetary destruction. Her wide smile spread clear across her face, showing her sharp teeth. Shouting loudly, so every Drone could hear. "This world is mine!"

Menzuo slammed his fist into the palm of his hand, violently. "She's going to pay for this!"

Just as he said that, Queen Eaziah opened her mouth, letting a pink fog seep out. It fell all the way down to the ground. The fog covered everything that was below.

As it started to rise, all the way back up to where she was, she began to speak. "The energy from Earth, along with the energy of all good and evil, will belong to planet Excervo. Queen Eaziah will reign supreme as this planet's ultimate ruler! Menzuo, you are a failure! This universe belongs to my wonderful husband, Lord Fetid!"

The last few humans who had not been captured were trying their best to get away from the rolling fog. As they did, they were easily caught by the Drones and shipped off of the planet. Within minutes, the entire city of Springfield was covered in a pink fog. The universal screen was completely blocked out by the pink mist.

King Zenshuo waved his hand from right to left, to make the screen disappear. The lights in the room slowly came back on. The panel continued to mumble with fear. The threat of Queen Eaziah was clear. Menzuo knew in his heart that their decision would be made out of fear. Not for the safety of the planet.

King Zenshuo slammed his gavel onto the table in front of him, to quiet the royal cabinet. "We have all witnessed what is taking place on Earth. Now, it is our duty as the royal, universal panel, to protect all life that resides under our reign. With our decision, we have to do what is best for the existing planets and the energy of all good and evil. We also must take into account another viable source of evil that is gaining strength in Hero City. The stability of Earth is not at its best," King Zenshuo looked over to Ambassador Naos as he watched him lower his head. "I am sorry to see your home in this condition, my old friend."

Naos couldn't speak. His thoughts were on his family and the humans that had been taken away from their world.

Allucio tugged on Nuncio's shirt. "What will happen next?" he whispered.

"I believe we are waiting for King Zenshuo's decision. Because he is taking so long, I do not believe that his decision will be good," Nuncio answered.

"I hope that it isn't bad," Desmurose responded.

"We can only hope," Nuncio followed.

After a few moments, King Zenshuo stood slowly from his chair. As he did, everyone in the royal conference room quieted. Menzuo and the others waited impatiently for his answer. "I vote...that Earth is destroyed immediately," the air in the room seemed to have left. It was all too quiet as he continued. "All remaining life on planet Earth will have twenty-four hours to find a way off before it is to be destroyed."

"What?" Menzuo shouted. Everyone in the crowd looked down at him.

Master Renzfly grabbed him by the arm. "No, Menzuo, you are not allowed to speak during the royal any meeting. Let the panel make the decision."

"But, how could he..." Menzuo retorted.

Master Renzfly quickly cut him off. "Quiet yourself quickly. Be patient."

Menzuo looked at Master Renzfly with tears in his eyes. He shook his head as he felt all too helpless. "I can't let him do that. That's my family out there," he snatched his arm away and walked forward. He stood in front of King Zenshuo's table and looked up. "My King, I cannot allow you to do this. The people of Earth deserve to have a safe planet. As I have heard, the life of slavery on planet Excervo is no way for anyone to live," King Zenshuo sat with a blank expression on his face. Menzuo continued. "I will protect Earth, with the help of my friends."

King Zenshuo looked down at his son. It was the first time in known history that someone had interrupted a verdict. "Young warrior, you are way out of line! You have no right to speak during this session.

"I am sorry, King Zenshuo," Menzuo said as he lowered his head.

Master Renzfly ran to his side. "Your highness, please forgive Prince Menzuo. He is very green to the rules of the universal panel. Please remove his remarks from the royal meeting's archives," he grabbed Menzuo's arm as tight as he could. "This will not happen again, my King," he jerked Menzuo's arm and led him back to the group.

"I am sorry, Master Renzfly, but I had to say something."

Master Renzfly looked deep into Menzuo's eyes, with anger. "I understand that you do not know the rules, but don't ever defy my words. That is not how any student of mine conducts himself.

Menzuo nodded. "Yes, Master," he stood next to his friends again.

The room was still quiet as they all waited for King Zenshuo to speak again. "Young Prince, it is too risky. You all have seen the Queen's powers. You all are not advanced enough in the ways of the Yardanian fighting style of protection, and there is absolutely no chance that any of you can save Earth. Even though you are marked as the universal protector, you stand no chance against the Queen. We must destroy Earth now."

The King from planet Pryzor stood up quickly and spoke without hesitation. "I second the motion to destroy planet Earth. It is for the greater good of the entire universe."

One after another, Kings and Queens stood up in favor of King Zenshuo's decision. Menzuo looked around with pain, quickly filling his heart. "How could you all act so quickly? I can beat her! I can beat her!" he shouted desperately.

The panel grew quiet as Ambassador Naos stood to his feet. "With all due respect to the universal panel, I have all faith in Menzuo to protect Earth. I am not speaking just because this is my home. I say this because I have faith in his ability and also in the spirit of his friends. Menzuo has fought for Earth's safety once and was victorious. Just recently, Menzuo and his friends have fought and saved planet Bralose from imminent destruction. As a strong team, I believe that they can do the same for planet Earth again."

King Zenshuo nodded to Ambassador Naos' suggestion and spoke to the rest of the panel. "Thank you for your comments, Ambassador Naos. If two more people stand by Ambassador Naos, Menzuo and the Solar Warriors will have their chance to protect planet Earth."

A few seconds passed as the panel sat quietly. All seemed to be lost, then suddenly, King Shovoh from planet Walonoke stood to his feet. "I am in favor of Ambassador Naos' decision. Prince Menzuo saved the former King, my father, from the deadly

Naleezar on planet Walonoke. Anyone who can deal with a beast should have the opportunity to battle for any planet's safety." He looked down at his father, Scoop, with a smile.

Scoop smiled back to his son, full of pride. He nodded with complete respect for his courage.

"One more nomination? Anyone? Anyone?" King Zenshuo shouted. No one else dared to stand up against the rest of the panel. As the King raised his gavel to reject the motion and to also end the meeting, the doors to the conference room flew open.

"I am in favor of Ambassador Naos' decision to have Menzuo and the Solar Warrior's, fight for Earth's safety," a person shouted loudly.

The rest of the panel mumbled with shock. Princess Amiata stepped forward with her eyes wide. "Father?" she said, surprised. "That sounds like my father," she looked around quickly. After a few seconds, she could see him, walking to his seat, with her mother. "That is him. He made it," she said happily to the others.

King Eojtaf and Queen Vanera looked down at their daughter, confidently and very happy to see her one more time.

King Zenshuo lowered his gavel and looked down to Menzuo, with a dull expression. He spoke with a lack of confidence. "You and your friends are allowed to return to Earth, Prince Menzuo, but remember if Earth is not safe within twenty-four hours, it will be destroyed."

Menzuo nodded as he looked into his father's angry eyes. He turned to Ambassador Naos. "We will not let you down."

Ambassador Naos nodded. Without a word spoken, walked out of the universal meeting room. Menzuo turned and walked passed everyone and out of the room as well. He met up with Ambassador Naos in the hallway. "I am proud of you, Menzuo, but you were way out of line. You have much to learn. As you can see, my objection to the final order, with the say of two other people on the royal panel, would have halted Earth's demise."

"I am sorry Ambassador Naos, but I was terrified that my father was going to blow up the planet, you sat so calm in there."

"That is because I know the process. I had nothing to fear until the final judgment had been set."

Menzuo lowered his head. "I am sorry for speaking out of line. I hope I didn't mess things up too much."

"You did, but I understand how you feel."

Menzuo sighed as he lifted his head again. "Ambassador Naos, is it really that bad in the city? Is the planet really in that much danger?"

Naos nodded with a dull look on his face. "It is far worse than what was seen in that room." he took a deep breath and let it out slowly. "I must tell you, there has been so much evil released in the past few years, that I'm not sure if the planet can be saved. Please understand that there is a solid chance that you will not succeed, but I believe in my soul that you can defeat the Queen. She is powerful, stronger than any of the Pirate Warriors that you have recently faced. Both Morbid and Hydrosion's energy put together are not even close to how powerful she can be." He leaned up against the wall. "This battle will be perilous for you all. If you guys don't succeed…"

Menzuo stopped him from speaking any further. "Ambassador Naos, do not think negatively. We will succeed. Planet Earth means a lot to my friends and me. We have a lot to lose as well. Earth is our home, and I will do whatever I have to, to save it."

Naos put his arm onto Menzuo's shoulder. "I wish that I could go with you, but if I do, I would be breaking several universal laws, so I leave the fate of Earth in your hands. Get our home back, young warrior. Make her safe again."

Menzuo nodded with confidence as the others walked out of the room. Master Renzfly was the last one to walk out. "King Zenshuo would like to speak to you before we leave," Master Renzfly said as he turned and walked down the hallway behind the rest of the Solar Warriors.

Menzuo watched Naos lead his friends out of the castle. He closed the doors and went into a separate room. Menzuo turned to Naos with a half frown. "I think Master Renzfly is very upset with me for speaking out."

A smirk fell across Naos' face. "He'll get over it. He's a powerful warrior who follows strict Yardanian and all universal laws. That's why he's a great Master."

Menzuo nodded. "I guess you're right. I have to speak to my father," he said as he walked back to the conference room door.

"Prince Menzuo," Naos said quickly. "Keep your head up. Everything will be just fine."

Menzuo nodded with respect, then opened the door. As he walked in, the last of the royal panel were walking out of the room. King Zenshuo was still sitting on his chair in the balcony. He looked down and noticed Menzuo standing in front of the doorway. "Close the door and step forward, young man."

Menzuo did precisely what his father said and walked cautiously to the center of the room. He looked up, noticing the anger residing on the King's face. "Yes, my King," he said quickly.

The place was quiet as King Zenshuo slowly leaned forward. Looking down at Menzuo, his face went blank. "Not in all my years as King of this planet and head representative of this universe, have I ever come across such a stubborn young warrior."

"But father, I..."

King Zenshuo jumped out of his seat. "You are not allowed to speak!" he shouted. Menzuo's eyes widened as he watched his father sit back down. As he lowered his head, the echo from the King's yell slowly faded. He continued. "Now, young warrior, even though you are my son, you must understand how the universal panel operates. If you are ever again invited to sit in on a universal order, you cannot speak. Unless you are sitting in one of these seats. Your voice cannot be heard. The royalty and ambassadors who sit here are very capable of making the hard decisions for this universe. Is that understood?"

"Yes, my King," Menzuo responded.

King Zenshuo sighed heavily. "Now that we have gotten that out of the way, I must say," Menzuo's head finally lifted. "I am proud of what you have done on Earth and also for saving planet Bralose. You are becoming a great warrior at such a young age, but you cannot let anger rise in you so easily. That is the path to weakness and to the destruction of any Yardanian Warrior. You must learn to fight with a pure heart and not with so much hate. If you continue to do so, you will not fulfill the destiny that is before you."

"Yes, father. May I please speak now?" Menzuo said respectfully.

"Yes, you may, my Prince."

Menzuo took a deep breath. "How am I supposed to fight without anger? It seems impossible when I am fighting such an evil force."

"That, I cannot tell you how to do. Not even Master Renzfly can give you that answer. You must find that within yourself,"

King Zenshuo stood from his seat once again. "Just try your best to keep your heart pure. Never let anger fill it, or the consequences of your actions will overtake the purity within your soul."

"Yes, father, I will do my best."

King Zenshuo started to walk to the exit. Be safe, my son." He said as he walked out of the conference room.

"He is a straightforward man, Menzuo," Solar said from inside of the blue diamond.

"I see. I've never met someone so stuck in his ways."

"Oh, really? I think you are standing in the skin of someone like that right now."

"Who, me? How can that be?" Menzuo said curiously.

"You and I are both of the same flesh. We are the King's children and just as stubborn. For you to jump up and speak out like that proves it."

Menzuo smiled. '"I guess so, Solar."

"Now c'mon, everyone is waiting for us."

"Right," Menzuo said. He took a deep breath and walked out of the room. He walked down the hallway and out of the castle. Everyone was standing at the bottom of the steps, ready to head into battle. Menzuo could see the urgency in their faces.

As Menzuo made his way down the castle steps, Nuncio looked into his eyes. "We are ready to go to my Prince."

Menzuo nodded. He looked at the rest of his friends earnestly. "If you do not want to go through this battle, I will understand. This is going to be a hazardous situation. I might not return, and I'm ready to face that fate. So this is your last chance to back out."

Everyone looked at Menzuo as Desmurose stepped forward. "Look, we have been friends since birth, and there is no way that anyone of us is going to leave your side now. I know that I speak for everyone when I say this, no matter where you go, we will be there."

Everyone stepped forward and stood next to Desmurose confidently. "He is absolutely right about that, Menzuo." Scoop said with just as much confidence.

"You should know better than to question us," Allucio stated. "We will always be by your side, no matter what, dawg."

Princes Amiata and Nuncio walked over to him. "As much as you have done for our planet, it would be a disgrace if we didn't return the favor," Amiata said with a half-smile.

"It is not in the Bralokian way to turn away from honoring our duties," Nuncio confirmed.

Solar reappeared from the blue diamond and stood next to Menzuo. He nodded happily. "There you have it. They are true Solar Warriors."

Menzuo nodded as he understood his friend's decision. "Then I guess we should get going."

Just before they got onto the ship, the doors to the castle busted open. Everyone turned around and noticed Master Renzfly walking towards them. Menzuo stepped away from everyone. "Yes, Master Renzfly? What is it?"

He looked at the group and then back to Menzuo. "It would be my honor to fight by your side. I cannot sit and watch you battle this beast without my assistance."

"But, I thought you were upset with me?"

"You are my student, and I expect you to make mistakes. I'll never give up on you."

Menzuo smiled and then looked back at Solar. "I think we just went one up in this battle, guys," Solar said as Menzuo and Master Renzfly walked to the ship together.

They all got in and floated into the sky. As the Solar Warriors did, Ambassador Naos walked out of the castle just in time to see them rise above the clouds. "Good luck, you all. Return order to Earth," the ship blasted out of planet Yardania and sped towards the inner realm.

Chapter 3

Planet in Despair

The Solar Warriors flew past most of the planets in the outer realm and quickly towards the vortex that led back to where Earth was. As they passed planet Excervo, everyone noticed the dark cloud that once covered it, was now gone. Excervo now bizarrely resembled Earth.

"Look, guys!" Desmurose pointed out quickly. The rest of the team leaned over to look out of the window.

"This is not good," Master Renzfly stressed. "We must hurry, time is running out."

Menzuo could tell that Excervo was quickly killing his home planet. With the concerned look on his Master's face, Menzuo knew that this battle would mean more than defeating the Queen.

"No problem Master Renzfly," Nuncio said forcefully. "Everyone strap in. I'm putting the ship into hyper-drive!"

Everyone quickly took their seats as the spaceship picked up speed. "We're ready, Nuncio," Master Renzfly shouted.

"Initiating hyper-drive!" Nuncio yelled. He slammed his hand down on the yellow button.

The ship blasted off, stretching the stars as it quickly reached the inner realm's vortex.

~Menzuo~

Before they knew it, the ship had flown through the joining realms vortex. Within seconds they were just minutes away from their destination. Planet Earth was in the distance, and they all could feel the pain that was being inflicted on her.

Nuncio released the hyper-drive as he noticed a strange fog covering the entire upper east coast of the United States. "That has to be where the Queen is."

"We can't even see all of New England, "Allucio said.

"This is unreal," Desmurose followed.

"Nuncio," Solar shouted quickly. "Park on Earth's moon, we need to figure out a way to get onto the planet undetected."

"No problem," Nuncio replied. He quickly turned the ship towards the moon.

They sat and looked out of the ship's windows at the swirling pink cloud, wondering what was happening on Earth. "How are we going to get on it? I know those Pirate Drones will be waiting for us," Menzuo snarled.

"I know," Allucio agreed. The spaceship slowly landed on the moon. The ship's nose was facing the Earth. "We have to find out if our parents were taken before we battle that beast."

Scoop stood from his seat. "I know of a way that we can get onto the planet without being detected."

Everyone turned to face him very curious about what he had to say, "Speak, King Scoop," Master Renzfly said anxiously.

"Well, we can use the Walonokian space travel jelly to get onto Earth. While we are all in the jelly, we can lower our powers. That way, we can bypass the Pirate Drones, undetected."

"Are you sure that will work?" Nuncio questioned.

Wyler stepped forward. "I am sure of it. That is the best way for all Walonokian's to travel from planet to planet. It works well with the whistlers, and it will work for us."

Menzuo smiled. "Good thinking, Scoop, and Wyler," he stood from his seat as well. "We need to go now!"

Everyone stood. "Hold on," Master Renzfly spoke, quickly catching the young warrior's attention. "From here on out, we will only be able to communicate with each other telepathically. This way, we can make sure that our voices cannot be heard."

Everyone nodded in agreement as they walked to the ship's door. Menzuo looked at Solar with a straight face. "Are you ready?"

Solar nodded. "Of course, I am. I'm always ready to protect and serve." he made himself turn into the ball of light. He quickly re-entered the blue diamond. "Let's get to it."

Menzuo cracked a smile as Scoop spoke. "Okay, everyone, hold out your arms, and close your eyes. This will only take a second." Everyone followed his instructions as Scoop moved his hands in a circular motion. "Cigam Leg Raeppa! (Magic Gel Appear!)."

In an instant, they were all covered in the Walonkian space jelly.

The door to the ship slowly opened, exposing them to space. The pink cloud seemed to thicken with color. Without a word. The team of warriors all slowly flew out of the ship one by one.

Master Renzfly spoke to them telepathically. "Okay, we are about to enter planet Earth. Before we do, I will make us all disappear by using the Sensing Densor. Lower your energy levels as soon as we hit that pink cloud. From there on, I'll take care of the rest." they all nodded and followed him towards Earth.

As they closed in on the thick pink cloud, Menzuo couldn't help but think about his family and all of his friends. He only wanted them to be safe, and he was willing to do whatever it took to make sure that happened.

~Menzuo~

A few moments later, the Solar Warriors entered the pink cloud. As they did, they all lowered their energy so that they would not be detected by the Drones or Queen Eaziah. "Sensing Densor!" Master Renzfly shouted, making them all disappear. "Now, this will not be a pretty sight, so try and hold your emotions."

Within seconds, the pink cloud started to thin. As soon as they broke through Earth's atmosphere, everyone could see the massacre that had fallen upon the city below.

"Oh, No!" Desmurose yelled telepathically as they all continued their free fall towards the ground. "What did these monsters do to our home?" he asked angrily as he watched the burning fields continue to produce thick black clouds of smoke.

Allucio turned his head to the left and noticed several demolished streets and crumbled buildings. "This is crazy!" he responded.

Master Renzfly spoke softly. "I know that it looks bad, but we can fix it," he paused for a minute as they fell closer to the ground. They passed several Drones, like missiles. They were utterly undetected. Master Renzfly noticed the field getting closer. "In a few seconds, I will make us reappear. When I do quickly power up and fly as fast as you can towards the land below."

Just before they reappeared, Menzuo felt something deep in his heart that made him look to his far left. "I feel our parents, guys!"

he yelled to Allucio and Desmurose. "Our street is over there to our left."

"Yeah, I feel them, too," Allucio responded.

"Yeah, me too!" Desmurose said as well.

Scoop looked to his left as he could feel the energy that resembled a human in distress. "They're about a few miles away. We can reach them quickly if we are careful."

"Release!" Master Renzfly shouted.

As everyone reappeared, they all shot down as close as they could to the ground. "Follow me!" Menzuo said as they flew just feet from the crumpled pavement below. Everyone followed behind him in line as they weaved through the rampaged streets of the New England town, doing their best to avoid being detected.

~Menzuo~

A few hundred miles later, Menzuo and the others found their street. It was demolished entirely. Nothing was like it used to be. Everyone landed on the sidewalk at the top of the road. Menzuo, Allucio, and Desmurose noticed that every home for miles around them had been destroyed. Along with the houses, the trees and anything else that may have been around them was utterly obliterated. As Menzuo's eyes fix upon where his home used to stand, he could see smoke billowing from the rubble. His heart started to beat faster. Allucio and Desmurose walked towards their houses with the same feeling flowing deep inside of them.

Scoop walked over to Menzuo as a tear fell from his face. "Menzuo, please try to calm yourself. I do not think that your parents are gone. I can feel their energy. It is very weak, but your parents are still alive," Scoop grabbed Menzuo's hand. "Just focus on the energy, you will feel it too."

Menzuo took a deep breath. He closed his eyes and started to focus on their energy. Within seconds, he could sense his parents, along with Allucio and Desmurose's parent's power. Menzuo's eyes quickly opened. "You're right, Scoop, they are alive. They are all still alive, but where are they? I remember speaking to Barkley in my sleep, but I can't remember where he took them. I just hope that we're not too late."

Everyone walked over to where he and Scoop were standing. Allucio and Desmurose pulled themselves together and made their way over as well. "Close your eyes once again, Menzuo, and concentrate," Scoop said as he held tight to his hand. "You will be able to see everything that has happened, leading up to the destruction of your home."

Menzuo took a deep breath and quickly closed his eyes again. He focused as hard as he could on their energy. As he did, the rest of the Solar Warriors stood next to him anxiously, waiting to hear the finding of what he was seeing.

A few moments later, Menzuo noticed a bright light that quickly went dim. He could see his parents in his house, sitting at the kitchen table with Allucio and Desmurose's parents. They were all drinking coffee and seemed to be having a great conversation. He noticed Barkley sleeping by the back door, calm as usual. This brought a smile to his face. "I see our parents', guys. They're in my kitchen talking," Menzuo said.

"Can you hear anything?" Allucio asked curiously.

"Hold on, I'll see if I can get anything," Menzuo answered, then tried to focus a little harder.

As he did, the sound of voices came in very clear. "I can't believe that happened!" Steven said as he hunched over from the laughter.

"I know," John O'Conner followed. "Yeah, Mary just watched that old man tell that lady off! She didn't know what to do."

"What did you do?" Michael Santiago responded.

"I just got out of that line and eased my way out of the store. I didn't want any part of that drama. That man looked like he was about to hit everybody in his range with that cane of his."

They all continued to laugh hysterically.

Menzuo smiled again. "They're talking and having fun. Just being our usual silly parents."

As they continued their conversation, the smile slowly left his face. "What do you see, Menzuo?" Desmurose questioned.

He saw Barkley jump up and run over to the back window. "Something is wrong!"

"What is it?" Desmurose said anxiously.

"I don't know yet," Menzuo said. He watched his father yell at Barkley, trying to make him stop growling. Steven jumped up from the table very angry and grabbed Barkley by the collar, but the dog wouldn't stop.

As soon as Steven looked into the sky, his face went pale. "My...my father, he saw something! Something terrible! I think it was Queen Eaziah." Menzuo retorted.

"What's going on? Please tell us!" Allucio and Desmurose yelled frantically.

"Wait! Something's happening!" Menzuo said, quickly grabbing everyone's attention. "Barkley is trying to back my dad away from the window."

With his hand still holding onto Barkley's collar, he led Steven down to the basement. 'C'mon!" Steven shouted. Everyone quickly followed closely behind him without question. As soon as they reached the bottom step, Barkley shook loose from Steven's grasp.

"What did you see, honey?" Krystal said as she could see her husband standing in complete shock.

"I don't know what that thing was, but it didn't look too good."

Without hesitation, Barkley moved a rug to the side. As he did, he revealed a hidden door. The dog scratched at it, indicating for Steven to open it.

"What is this? I never knew that there was a door down here?" Steven said curiously.

Barkley continued to bark and scratch at the door. "I think he wants you to open it," Michael Sr. said quickly.

A rumbling sound shook the house. Screams from people outside could be heard as they ran for cover. "Hurry!" Krystal shouted.

Steven pulled as hard as he could, but the door wouldn't budge. "It's not moving! I think it's stuck!"

John and Michael quickly moved in to help. "Pull on three," Michael shouted. "One–Two–Three!"

As they all pulled, the door lifted from the floor. A breeze of cold air hit their parent's faces. As they looked down, they all noticed stairs leading into the darkness. Barkley quickly ran down. "C'mon, follow the dog," Steven shouted. The ladies went in first. Steven was the last one in. He reached for the latch and slammed the door shut. Just as he closed it, they all heard the house explode.

The sound shocked Menzuo, making his eyes open quickly. With a terrified expression on his face, he took a deep breath. "They're in a hidden room under the basement. Barkley saved them."

"C'mon! Their air is probably running out in that room!" Allucio said as he and the others quickly picked up pieces of the house.

They tossed the wood and bricks out of their way. The noise of the debris hitting the ground alerted the Pirate Drones that were in the area of the team's presence. Master Renzfly could feel the Drones energy getting more robust. "We must hurry, they now know that we are here."

A few seconds later, Menzuo shouted. "There it is! The door is right there!" he quickly pulled the door out of the ground and threw it across the street. When he looked into the hole, he noticed all of their parents and Barkley, lying motionless in the hole.

"They're knocked out. We have to get them out of there fast," Desmurose said as they all rush down."

The screams from the Pirate Drones grew louder. They were getting closer.

Wyler and Scoop turned and looked towards the ends of the street. They're here, guys. They're coming quick!" Wyler responded.

"C'mon everyone, we have to get them out of there," Menzuo said. "Everyone, grab someone. I'll get Barkley."

"Rrraaack! Rrraaack! Rrraaack!" The growls of each Pirate Drone grew louder as Menzuo and the others emerged.

"Whoa! There are so many of them coming!" Princess Amiata shouted as she looked at the black flood of Drones heading towards them.

"Everyone, grab hold to me now!" Master Renzfly shouted. "Hurry!" Everyone held onto a part of his body. He closed his eyes as the Pirate Drones were just a few feet away. "Mega Sensing Densor!" Master Renzfly shouted as loud as he could.

In an instant, the Solar Warriors disappeared, leaving the Drones standing in a circle, very confused, and wondering what happened to their enemies.

As the Solar Warriors quickly vanished off of the planet, a Prince Drone made his way over to Queen Eaziah as she floated high over the city. "My Queen," the Prince Drone said as he lowered his head with respect. "The young warrior, Prince Menzuo, has returned to the planet. He came to rescue his parents, and he is not alone. He has come with several followers who may become a problem."

Queen Eaziah floated with her eyes closed as she focused on Menzuo's energy. She couldn't detect where it was coming from, but she could tell that he was near. "Mmm, a problem, my sweet? Never that. The young ignorant fools who have decided to travel with Prince Menzuo aren't anything of the sort. They are merely sport in the game of war. I will leave them to you and the rest of the Drones. That problem will be solved with over a million answers."

The Prince Drone raised his head. "Yes, my Queen. I understand. I will call every Drone to stay ready for war. These foolish warriors will be flooded with pain if they decide to return."

Queen Eaziah ran her tongue across her sharp teeth. "Oh, they will return. Those lovelies do not know the meaning of failure, and I will be glad to introduce them to it. Get my children ready for battle."

Prince Drone nodded. "Yes, my Queen," he flew off to round up his Drone brothers to ready them for a pure massacre.

"You can open your eyes now," Master Renzfly said softly.

Solar flew out of the blue diamond and stood next to Menzuo. As everyone opened their eyes, they noticed that they were back on the space ship. "How did you do that?" Desmurose said curiously.

"Don't worry, you will learn it one day," Master Renzfly replied.

"Why couldn't we just do that to get to Earth? It seemed easy enough to use?" Allucio said.

Master Renzfly took in an intense breath. "Using that technique can only be used to return to a place of safety or back to battle. As long as I have visited the place in my physical state, I can always return."

"Oh, I see, but that was cool!" Allucio responded.

Menzuo placed Barkley onto a seat as everyone slowly placed the others down on chairs. Solar walked over to the parents and put his hands on them to revitalize their strength.

Menzuo stroked Barkley's head as he lay unconscious. "Good dog. Thank you, buddy."

Princess Amiata put her hand on the young Prince's shoulder. "They will be okay, Menzuo. Nothing is going to happen to them up here."

Menzuo slowly stood and nodded with confidence. He took a deep breath as he looked at everyone with a stern expression. "Alright, it's time to get to work. Our city is destroyed. Our friends have been taken and made slaves on threat horrible planet, and there is no telling what they are going through right now," he clenched his fists tightly as he looked at his friends. "If we don't fix this, then you know the final outcome. We must save those people and the planet."

"We will not fail, Prince Menzuo," Allucio said with a straight face. "We have no choice but to succeed."

"No matter what," Desmurose added.

Menzuo nodded again. He quickly focused his attention on Master Renzfly. He grabbed onto his hand. "Send us all back to where we left those beasts."

"We are the Solar Warriors, and we will make them remember our names for all eternity!" Solar said, boosting everyone's confidence. He made his body hollow once again and re-entered the stone.

Everyone placed one hand on a part of Master Renzfly's body. He looked at them without breaking a smile. "Make them pay for all that they have done. Now close your eyes." they all followed his directions then lowered their heads. "Mega Sensing Densor!"

In that instant, the Solar Warriors vanished from the ship and headed back into battle with the Drones and to face the deadly Queen Eaziah.

Chapter 4

Queen Eaziah's Surprise

As the Pirate Drones continued to stand around in total confusion, they all looked at each other, trying their best to figure out what had happened to the warriors. They slowly started to move away from the area, a rush of energy made the wind pick up. The Drones froze and looked around to see where the surge was coming from.

In that moment of confusion, Menzuo and the others quickly reappeared, catching every one of them off guard. "Mega Body Attack!" Menzuo shouted.

He quickly blasted hundreds of the Drones out of his way, leaving a path past the end of the street.

As the other Drones realized what just happened, they refocused on the returned warriors and were ready to continue their attack. Desmurose yelled quickly. "Menzuo, go and find Queen Eaziah. We'll handle these monsters."

Menzuo nodded. "Got it! Make them all pay," he flew high into the sky.

The Pirate Drones watched the young Prince fly away without any care. They concentrated their attacks on their enemies that stood in front of them. "Rrraaack! Rrraack! Rrraaack!" Over and over, they growled and screamed, waiting for one of the young warriors to expose themselves to an attack.

"Don't give them a second to breathe," Princess Amiata shouted over the growls. "Make them pay!" she held her hands up and balled her fists as tight as she could. A soft beam of light formed over her body. "Aaah!" she yelled as she charged into the crowd. Without hesitation, she was hitting every Drone that stood in her way. As she did, the ones that she touched turned into the black ooze and disappeared from the streets.

The rest of the Solar Warriors started in on their attacks, beating the swarm of Pirate Drones into the same type of ooze. The war had just begun, and the young warriors were not going to give in.

As his friends fought off the Drones, Menzuo continued to fly high into the sky. He looked down to see how they were doing. He noticed that his friends were doing a great job holding the Drones off with their furious attacks.

The Solar Warriors punches and kicks echoed high into the sky, alerting the other Drones to make their way to the battle.

"Beat them all down! Make every last one of those disgusting Drones pay for coming to Earth," Menzuo said as he continued to fly high above the ground. He continued to search for the Queen. As he flew higher, a sharp pain quickly hit him in the stomach. He knew exactly who it was. His face turned as anger filled within him. "I'm coming, Eaziah! I've been waiting for this. Your threat is over," he flew to the west towards her, ready to battle.

As he sped through the sky at a lightning pace, he noticed a woman standing on a mountain in the distance. The lady had two long horns coming from her head. Long purple and orange-colored hair, draped over her shoulder that ran down to her waist. A tight red dress squeezed against her body, showing her muscular physique. Menzuo could feel the energy flowing from her, and it grew more reliable the closer he flew towards her. "I know it's her," Solar said as Menzuo slowed.

"Get ready to meet your maker!" Menzuo shouted.

"Be careful, Menzuo, she is mighty," Solar said, trying his best control the Prince's anger. "Don't let your emotions get the best of you."

Menzuo took a deep breath and slowly regained control of himself. "Okay, Solar. It's good to have you with me," Menzuo responded.

As the young warrior flew closer to the Queen, she held her arms out and smiled happily. "Oh my dear, Prince Menzuo," she shouted. "I was wondering when you were going to show. I knew that you had returned to this good-for-nothing planet. I knew the second you broke through its atmosphere," she lifted herself into the sky and floated a few feet above the mountain. She continued. "That is why I called all of my children to kill your friends. This was all planned. Your friends will never last. There are far too many Drones on this planet, such a pity."

"Why are you doing this?" Menzuo asked curiously.

"It is what I love to do. When you destroyed my sons, Morbid and Hydrosion, I had no choice but to step in. I told Lord Fetid that there was no need for him to send another Pirate, I wanted the joy of defeating you. My brave sons did a great job letting you believe that you were the 'all-mighty' universal protector, but you have to understand, honey, I am the real threat."

"You and your kind are disgusting. Why would you want to do this to the people on this planet?"

Eaziah shrugged her shoulders. "Hey, we're only out to have fun as we wreak havoc throughout the universe. You see, the Drones get much joy out of conquering small worlds, but I get pleasure by taking over this universe. Once I am finished with you and your measly team of fools, I will get a hold of the energy of all good and evil. Once that has been accomplished, I will make my husband the most feared Lord throughout this universe."

Menzuo balled his fists in anger as he continued to think. He slowly relaxed. A smirk fell upon his face, confusing the Queen. "That's very sad that you bow down to a man. Why aren't you the one in control? You're doing all of the work."

"My place is not to rule alone," she said, then floated higher into the sky. "Lord Fetid knew that you were getting too confident and way too powerful for any other Pirate to fight off. He knew that he had to send the second most powerful Pirate, that being me, to finish you off. He cannot leave Excervo at this point in time. If my Lord leaves, our planet will be open to being destroyed by the Yardanian forces." She swung her hair to her other shoulder. The wind caught hold of it. "You see, your birth father and my husband are the balancing forces in this universe. Their energy is linked to their home planets. That is why we are here battling for supremacy and not them. Neither one of them can allow that risk, but soon enough, that will not matter. You will be defeated, and the Yardanian threat will end."

"So, what will happen when I win?" Menzuo asked confidently.

"You win, my dear boy? You have no idea what you are up against. You will not win. It just is not possible. Plus, I have already given Excervo a nice gift. I know that you and your friends noticed the change."

Menzuo thought for a second. "Yeah, the black cloud was disappearing. Why?"

Queen Eaziah smiled. "Well, Prince Menzuo," she said as she floated closer to him. "As we speak, I am draining Earth's energy. These worthless humans are becoming slaves on my planet, and soon enough, we will be able to take over planet Yardania. There is nothing that you can do about it."

"I believe that you are mistaken. I will beat you, and I will save Earth. I will not fail."

Queen Eaziah crossed her arms and continued to smile. "Well, since you think that you are the universes savior, I'll give you a chance to protect it," the wind picked up and blew her dress and hair, making it flow like the ocean. "Give it your best shot!"

Menzuo powered up, making the wind blow her hair and dress back more violently. "No problem!" he shouted as he quickly charged toward her. As he swung at Queen Eaziah's face, her smile widened.

The sound of his punches echoed like thunder. Without hesitation, he continued his attack, punching her in the face and stomach as hard as he could. Each blow shook the planet.

The entire time that Menzuo attacked the Queen, the smile never left her face. His punches and kicks seemed to have no effect.

"Ha, ha, ha, ha!" Queen Eaziah laughed at his efforts. "My dear boy, what do you think you are doing?"

Menzuo quickly stopped as her laughter grew louder. The young Prince was very agitated. He built up all of the energy in his body. A glow covered his hands like they were dipped in gold. "Let's see if you can laugh at this! Mega body attack!"

Three massive fireballs flew from his hands, directly towards Queen Eaziah. "Ha, ha, ha, ha!" she continued to laugh as the fireballs flew closer to her.

The blast sent her down towards the mountain and directly through it, leaving a massive cloud of dust in the wake.

"I can still sense her energy, Menzuo; it's growing stronger. Be careful," Solar shouted cautiously.

It was silent for a moment, but her laughter strengthened as she reappeared from the dust below. "Ha, ha, ha, ha!"

"That's it! I've had it with her!" Menzuo shouted as he noticed her standing just below him. He flew higher into the sky. Menzuo could still hear the evil Queens' laughter. "She's going to pay for this! Aaah!"

In that instant, the young warrior shot down towards her like a missile.

As he did, she floated up towards him, still laughing at his attempts to destroy her. "What do you have for me now, my poor little Prince?"

Just as she said that the blue diamond brightened. "Something's happening, Menzuo!" Solar yelled, but Menzuo wasn't paying attention.

At that moment, Menzuo's body turned into a brightly lit diamond-shaped sword. As Eaziah noticed Menzuo flying towards her, she held out her arms as if she was waiting to embrace him.

Menzuo flew right through her, cutting the Queen at the waist, leaving her torso and legs floating next to each other.

Menzuo stopped himself from flying and landed on the ground. The laughter stopped as Menzuo's body went back to normal. "I think she's done Solar," Menzuo responded to the silence.

As he looked into the sky, Menzuo noticed the split that he caused. "Great job, Menzuo," Solar said confidently, "Now let's finish her off and save this planet."

Menzuo nodded then floated back into the sky right in front of her face. "I thought you said that I couldn't defeat you? It looks like you were wrong, just like your children. It's over, you ugly beast."

As Menzuo said that, Queen Eaziah slowly picked her head up. "It's not over, my little Prince. You have just released the better half of me," she said with a wide smile.

Menzuo backed away, shaking with confusion. "How is she alive? I can't believe this!"

A few seconds later, a pink cloud flew from her waist and from her torso. "Oh no, Menzuo! She's getting stronger. Her power is unbelievable," Solar shouted.

Menzuo looked on as he was still in complete shock. "This is going to be beautiful!" Queen Eaziah shouted as the pink cloud covered both parts of her body.

"No, no, this can't happen!" Menzuo screamed angrily.

The pink cloud slowly disappeared, and there stood two Queens, one in a blue dress, and the other in red. Welcome, my sister. We have some beautiful work to finish," the blue Queen said.

"Ooh! That sounds so, so lovely," the red Queen responded as she stretched her arms out.

They both looked at Menzuo as he floated in amazement. "What a wonderful gift you have given me, young Prince," the blue Queen said softly, "You have definitely unleashed my beauty into this universe."

As their hair blew with the wind, Menzuo could feel both of their powers rising far beyond his. "This isn't good at all," Solar said in a very shaky voice.

"Ha, ha, ha!" their laughter grew louder by the second as their mouths opened, showing their sharp teeth. As Menzuo shook in fear, their horns started to glow.

At that moment, every Pirate Drone that was battling the Solar Warriors quickly stopped and looked into the sky. They all could sense the Queens' strength, and so could the others. "Oh no!" Master Renzfly shouted.

"What is that? The energy is unbelievable!" Nuncio shouted as he kept his guard up.

"It's the Queen. She has become stronger, more powerful than all of us put together. This is not good for any of us."

All of the Pirate Drones floated away from them, leaving the helpless warriors standing in their places. As soon as the cloud of Drones cleared the sky, they saw Menzuo floating in front of two figures. "No! This can't be!" Master Renzfly shouted.

"How can there be two of them?" Allucio asked in a shaky voice, but no one responded.

A few seconds later, they all felt the Earth shake, and two Queens' yelled out. "The end is now! Begone, you insulant fighters!"

The blue Queen quickly moved in and grabbed Menzuo by the neck. He had no chance to react to her movement.

"No, Menzuo!" Scoop screamed frantically.

"Let's go!" Princess Amiata yelled. She shot up into the sky towards Menzuo. The others quickly followed.

As they flew towards their friend, the red Queen quickly appeared in their path, smiling lovingly. She stopped them, instantly blocking their way. "So, my lovelies, where do you think you're going?" she asked as she rubbed her tongue over her sharp teeth. "Don't you want to see the pain that your beautiful little Prince is about to feel? Just stay there and watch. I would like for all of you to see what is about to happen to you."

They knew that she was way more powerful than all of them put together. They had no choice but to float and watch what the other Queen was about to do to their friend.

"Why can't we just take her on?" Desmurose asked.

"It would be of no use. We are at Eaziah's Mercy," Master Renzfly responded.

Desmurose clenched his teeth and tightened every muscle in his body as he looked at his friend.

"You had your chance, Prince Menzuo," the blue Queen said as her smile left her face. "Now it is time for you to die!" she punched Menzuo as hard as she could in his stomach, knocking the wind out of his body.

She continued to punch him over and over until his body was limp in her grasp. "Poor fool, I'm nowhere near finished with you. You will feel the worse pain ever inflicted on a warrior before I let you die," she said as she let Menzuo's limp body fall to the ground. As he fell, Queen Eaziah spread her arms wide and yelled. "Massacre of rage!"

In an instant, a vast blue wave flew from her body and covered Menzuo, making his body pause just inches from the ground.

"Oh, you are going to love this!" the red Queen said to the rest of the Solar Warriors.

The blue Queen spun counter-clockwise, making her horns light up the sky. As she did, the blue wave that covered Menzuo started to shrink.

"Aah, aah, noo!" Menzuo screamed as he was in complete pain. The blue wave was crushing his body.

The blue Queen stopped spinning and shot down towards him like a missile. Menzuo was helpless. "Fury attack!" the blue Queen shouted.

At that moment, an orange flame flew from her horns directly into the blue wave. The sky was filled with blue and orange slime! The Queen disappeared, and so had Menzuo.

"Where are they?" Wyler asked as they looked to the ground. There was nothing there, not even a hole where they last saw Prince Menzuo.

The red Queen laughed. "Ha, ha, ha, ha! Look behind you."

As they did, they saw the blue Queen smashing Menzuo's unconscious body into the last standing buildings in downtown

Springfield. Over and over, she continued to pummel his limp body. Each time his body slammed into a building, it shook the earth violently.

"That's it!" Desmurose yelled. "I can't take it anymore!" he shot off towards Menzuo as the blue Queen threw him into City Hall.

"No, Desmurose, stop!" Master Renzfly screamed, but it was too late.

In an instant, the red Queen appeared in his way. "No, no, no, my little friend, you must watch. No helping."

"Forget that!" Desmurose shouted angrily. He swung at her head. His punch landed right on the nose, sending her head back violently.

As she brought her face back in front of his, the smile left her face. "You little fool! How dare you hit me! Take this!"

In a flash, Desmurose was hit with an immense amount of energy. His body slammed into the mountain where the Queen once was, making it crumble.

"Why did you have to do that?" Master Renzfly shouted.

"Because I can," she responded. At that moment, she felt something in her stomach. She took a deep breath and let it out slowly. The Queen closed her eyes and smiled. As she opened them, she looked at the warriors happily, "It is time for all of you to die. Your little Prince is hanging on by the last bit of strength left in his body, and we are about to take it all out. It is time for all of you to join him."

"What is she doing?" Amiata asked curiously.

"I do not know," Master Renzfly responded.

As she opened her eyes again, she looked at the warriors with a happy expression gleaming on her face. "There is no need to resist your deaths. Goodbye my lovely warriors."

Master Renzfly's energy level shot through the planet. "Not if I can help it!" he shouted. "Let's go!" he quickly charged towards her. Everyone followed closely behind.

Before they were inches from the red Queen, she screamed. "Massacre of rage!" in an instant, they were all covered in the same purple wave that had surrounded Menzuo. The red Queen spun counter-clockwise, making her horns light up. The purple wave started to shrink around all of their bodies.

"Aah, aah, aah!" everyone screamed. The breath was quickly and painfully squeezed out of the Solar Warriors.

"Goodbye, little warriors! Fury attack!" an orange flame flew into the purple wave. At that exact moment, the red Queen flew in and joined her attack inside of the power stream.

Master Renzfly, Princess Amiata, and the other fighters were scattered all over the city. The sky was filled with blue and orange slime. The Solar Warrior's energy had been depleted.

The red Queen slowly floated over to her sister. She looked down at Menzuo's depleted body as it lay in the ruins of City Hall. "Great job, my sister," the red Queen said softly.

"Thank you. I see that you have disposed of our other little friends. That is wonderful," the blue Queen responded.

"Oh, of course, honey. These fools were not a problem at all. Sadly, they were so weak, though. It was nothing but light work for me. I didn't even get a chance to have any fun."

"Drones, gather the bodies, and bring them all back to us. It is time to send our lovelies to the death world of Legerdamien." the blue Queen yelled passionately.

Many of the Drones flew off across the city and gathered the warrior's energy depleted bodies.

A short while later, all of the Solar Warriors were lying on the crumbled steps of Springfield's City Hall, next to Menzuo. "How sad this is? Poor little so-called protectors, the battle never had a chance to get started," the red Queen spoke. She looked to all of the drones. "The universe now belongs to Lord Fetid!"

Thousands of Drones cheered loudly as they jumped up and down amid their victory. The two Queens raised their hands to quiet them. As the Drones went silent, the Queens held hands and looked down at the unconscious warriors. "Goodbye forever. Enjoy your time on Legerdamien. Say hello to Morbid and

Hydrosion for me, I know that they will be happy to see you, Menzuo," the blue Queen said.

"This universe is no longer your home," the red Queen added.

Both Queens opened their mouths as wide as they could. "Eeyaah! Eeyaah!" they both screamed.

A pink smoke poured out from their mouths and covered the warriors completely. "Resting blast!" they both shouted.

The ground rumbled violently. Unknown to the Queens, inside of the pink smoke, the blue diamond started to glow. It formed a force field around all of the Solar Warriors.

The pink smoke exploded instantly. Many of the Drones jumped back as the blast filled the sky. "It is done, my sister." The blue Queen said as she was filled with joy.

As the smoke faded, there was no trace of the mighty protectors. "They are dead! Forever gone! Forever gone!" the Queens yelled.

"Hoorah, hoorah, hoorah!" the Drones cheered happily.

Both Queens faced each other as they held hands. "Earth is now ours!"

Both Queens knew that with the Solar Warriors out of the picture, nothing would be able to stop their reign of terror. Mission number one was complete, now the search for the energy of all good and evil was their only task left to be completed.

~Menzuo~

Barkley was the first to wake up on the space ship. He was very groggy as he made his way to his feet. "Oh, boy, where am I?" Barkley said to himself. As his eyesight fully cleared, he noticed that he was in a very unfamiliar place, and that his Masters and friends were still unconscious. "I think we're still alive, but how?" he shook his head then walked over to Steven as he sat motionless on a chair.

Barkley jumped onto his lap and licked his face. "Huh? What's going on?" Steven said as he slowly woke. Barkley continued to lick his face until he was fully conscious. Steven's eyes finally opened, making Barkley stop. "Hey," he said as he looked around. "Where...where am I?" he sat forward as Barkley jumped down. He held his head as it was still hurting from the sound of the blast. Steven looked around, very curious about what he was seeing.

As Barkley tried to wake Krystal, Steven walked over to one of the windows. He looked out and noticed the sky was black, and a pink cloud was floating in the distance. "Where could I be?" Steven wondered. He then looked at the ground below and noticed several craters. Steven quickly jumped with shock. "I'm on the moon!" His mouth dropped as he looked at the pink cloud. "Is that Earth?" his screams echoed through the ship.

Everyone slowly woke up after hearing the scream. "What's going on?" John shouted as he shook his head, trying to clear his vision.

"Look! Look! We're not on Earth anymore! I think we're dead!" Steven said frantically.

Krystal jumped up as she regained consciousness. "We're dead? How can this be?" she ran over to Steven just as confused.

"Wait a minute," Michael Sr. said. "We're not dead. We're just not on Earth anymore."

Steven and Krystal quickly turned around and noticed everyone else sitting in their seats with sad expressions on their faces. "What's going on? Do you guys know something?"

Stacy sat back in her seat. "I think you guys better sit down for this," she wiped her face. "It's very complicated."

Steven and Krystal sat back down as Barkley made his way over to them. "Good dog. You saved us, but how did you know about that passageway? We've been in that house for years, and we never knew that it was there."

"Well," Marianne said with a half-smile. "Many things aren't what they seem to be, and your dog knows a lot more than you give him credit for."

"What are you talking about, Mary?" Krystal asked curiously.

"Should we tell them?" John said to the group.

"We can tell them what is happening on Earth, but we'll leave the rest to Menzuo to explain. It's only right."

"What's happening on Earth?" Steven asked. He was perplexed, "and what the heck is a Menzuo?"

John leaned forward. "Earth is being attacked by a very vicious beast."

"Yeah, I saw that thing flying in the sky. What was that?" Steven asked.

"It is called a Pirate Warrior. Actually, it was the Queen Pirate sent here to enslave all humans and literally destroy Earth's existence."

"Pirate Warrior?" Krystal said. "Sent from where?"

"From planet Excervo," Stacy added with a straight face.

"Planet Excervo? There's no such planet in this universe," Steven said as he sat back.

"There is Steven," Michael Sr. responded. "This universe is much bigger than what you may think it is. Everything that we have told you is true, and our home planet is in serious danger."

Steven lowered his head. Something quickly hit him. "Oh, my goodness! Where are the kids? Jammal! Jeffery! Michael!" he yelled frantically. He ran over to the window and looked at the pink cloud. "We have to save them!"

"Relax, they are fine," Marianne responded.

Krystal lifted her head as Steven made his way back to his seat. "What do you mean, they are okay? If they are on Earth, then they are in danger. They're only kids for goodness sake."

"They are not regular kids' guys," Stacy said. "They are not from this planet."

Steven and Krystal sat up in complete confusion. They couldn't speak as they looked at the O'Conner's and Santiago's.

"You see guys, we're not from planet Earth and your son Jammal isn't either," Michael Sr. spoke.

Steven's eyes widened. "What? Can you say that again?"

Michael leaned forward. "We're all from a planet known as Yardania, situated in the outer realm of our universe. Our children, as well as your son, originate from that planet. It is a planet of protector warriors."

"Your son Jammal's real name is Menzuo. He is a warrior that was sent to Earth to protect it from evil if it were to ever reach here," John said. "Your son is actually Yardanian royalty."

Steven shook his head. "I can't believe a word of this. This must be some type of joke."

"I know," Krystal followed. "How can this be real? Our son, a Prince, a warrior?" she shook her head as well. "This just can't be. I don't believe you."

"Okay, if you don't believe us, then press that blue button over there on the dashboard," John said as he pointed to the button.

Steven turned around and looked at it in confusion. "You mean that button? I don't want to blow up the ship."

"You won't, just push it," Michael Sr. said.

Steven walked over to the front seats and sat down. He slowly reached out and tapped the blue button. A white screen quickly appeared over the front window. He jumped back as a woman's soft voice spoke out. "You have activated the biography of our Yardanian Prince, Menzuo."

"What is this?" Steven said with a startled voice.

"Just watch and listen," Marianne answered.

On the screen, appeared three Pirate Drones, sneaking into a child's room. As they moved towards the crib, they tripped an alarm and were instantly surrounded by four royal guards. The fighting woke the baby, alerting more guards to their side. As the battle went on, the voice continued. "On this night, our beloved Prince was almost abducted by Lord Fetid's Drones. This event weighed heavily on our King and Queen. They both made the decision to send their child, their only living son, to the safest planet within the universe. He would be far from the evil Pirate of planet Excervo. It was decided that baby Menzuo would be sent to planet Earth…"

Steven and Krystal sat in awe as they looked at Jammal's birth parents, holding him. The tears running from their eyes showed the deep pain of letting go of their son. Soon after, the vision on the screen changed, showing Menzuo being placed into a capsule. The lid slowly closed. Menzuo's mother kissed it gently and waved goodbye. Within seconds, the small ship shot out of the planet and quickly headed towards Earth.

Steven shook his head in disbelief. "This is unreal."

The woman's voice that told Menzuo's story continued. "Upon Menzuo's journey to Earth, a Yardanian spy alerted planet Excervo of King Zenshuo's plan. With this information on hand, Lord Fetid sent his most ferocious Pirate to Earth to destroy Menzuo and to crush the royal Yardanian bloodline. The sinister Pirate Warrior, Morbid, quickly headed for planet Earth. As the news came to King Zenshuo about the Yardanian spy, he knew that he had to do whatever it took to protect his son. Being a brilliant King, our Lord not only sent his son to the safest planet within the universe, but King Zenshuo also counteracted Morbid's mission. He sent a protective force field to the planet with his son. With this given energy, upon Menzuo's twelfth birthday, our Prince's destiny would be put into place. Our young warrior would be ready to face Morbid. If he succeeded, he would be able to develop into a great warrior and serve as planet Earth's protector," the screen faded as so did the woman's voice.

Steven's eyes were as wide as they could get.

"You see," Stacy said, "Everything that you are experiencing right now is all true."

Krystal sat back in the seat and covered her eyes. "I can't believe this is happening to us. Our son is the protector of Earth?"

Marianne walked over and sat in the chair next to her. "Not just Earth," she said as she placed her hand onto Krystal's leg, "He is also the protector of this entire universe."

Krystal's head quickly popped up. "But that is not what the lady on the screen said."

"I know," Marianne responded. "That screen isn't updated to the present time. Many things have changed since Menzuo's...I mean, Jammal's arrival. His inner energy and life's prophecy was given to him, and he found out that he is the chosen one."

Krystal's head slowly dropped back into her hands. "Oh, this is so wonderful," she said sarcastically.

"It will be okay," Susanne said softly. "It just takes a while to let it sink in."

Steven looked out towards planet Earth once again. "What have we gotten ourselves into, honey?"

Michael Sr. reached into his pocket and pulled out a bag of dust and poured a little into the palm of his hands. He walked over to Steven and Krystal. "I think it will be best if both of you rested until we got back on Earth."

Steven looked at Michael, confused. "Got back on Earth? It looks like it's going to be gone soon," he looked at Michael's hand. "What is that?"

"Just a little something to put you both at ease," he blew the orange dust into Steven and Krystal's face.

"Why are you blowing dust on me? Don't you know I'm allergic to..." he said quickly.

As both of them inhaled the dust, their bodies slowly relaxed. Krystal slouched further into her seat. "This can't be for real," she said in a soft tone. Her eyes slowly closed.

Steven hunched over in his seat as his eyes grew heavy. "My son, he's just a little boy. I hope that he is okay?" within seconds, his eyes were fully closed.

"He is," George said. "They all will all be just fine...we hope."

Steven and Krystal were now fully asleep on the spaceship. Everyone else sat back in their seats quietly as they looked at the stars as they brightened the sky. The vision of Earth covered in the pink cloud really bothered them, but they knew that it would be best to leave it in their children's hands.

Earth was under complete attack, and the Hall's had just gotten a lesson that they would never forget.

Chapter 5

Arrival to Legerdamien

A few moments later, the Solar Warriors appeared on their backs, unconscious on planet Legerdamien. The sky was pitch black, with only specs of light shining through the thick dark clouds. The musk of death and pain filled the moist air.

Menzuo was the first to wake. "What happened?"

As he spoke, Solar exited from the diamond. "Whoa! The Queen, she is way too powerful. I have never felt energy like that," he said as he looked at Menzuo.

The young Prince grabbed his head as he blinked slowly, trying his best to clear his vision. "I can't believe that we lost. I thought we had her beat."

"Me too, my Prince," Solar responded, "But that's the funny thing about each battle. They are very unpredictable until they are truly over."

Menzuo looked around. The thin beams of light brightened the ground below just enough so they could see a few feet in front of them. "Where are we?"

Solar took a deep breath as he looked around. "It looks and smells…like we're on Legerdamien, the warriors' death world."

Menzuo tried to stand, but he was still weak from the battle. "Well, that's just great!" He looked to his left and noticed everyone else still lying motionless. "Are the others okay, Solar?"

He looked to them as well. Focusing on their energy, he could tell how they felt. "I think so, but they are still out cold. I guess the Queen's really wanted to get rid of them, too. They wanted no threats around as they searched for the energy of all good and evil."

Menzuo tried to stand once again, this time he was able to. He looked at his hands and rubbed his legs. "How are we still alive?"

Solar pointed to the blue diamond. "Somehow, in some way, this blue diamond saved us. I could feel the energy surge through me as we were lying on the ground. I don't know what it was, but it is the only thing that could have saved us."

Menzuo sighed. "At least something did. Let's try to find a way out of here. Maybe we can find a way before everyone wakes. We have to get back to Earth somehow. We can't leave Queen Eaziah to do what she wants."

At that moment, Menzuo and Solar shot up into the sky and headed straight for the clouds, hoping to find an exit.

After a few seconds, a cold breeze blew over the Solar Warriors. Scoop and Wyler were the next to wake. They sat up, shook their heads, and looked around very confused. "Oh man, what happened?" Scoop asked, still trying to regain his focus.

"I think we're dead," Wyler responded. "We're not on Earth anymore."

They both slowly tried to stand. Wyler and Scoop's bodies were still wobbly. Scoop grabbed hold of his head. "I don't think we're dead, Wyler. I can still feel the pain from that disgusting Queen."

"Yeah, maybe you're right," Wyler answered as he noticed the others still lying unconscious. "Scoop, let's see if we can revive them."

"Okay, hold out your hands," Scoop said. They both held out their hands and generated the energy to their palms. "I'm still weak."

"We have to try," Wyler encouraged his best friend.

Scoop took a deep breath. "Okay, I'll give it my best."

As they did, they were both able to generate just enough energy to send to the other Solar Warriors. Slowly they all started to wake.

"Uh! Uh! Ouch!" they all groaned as they opened their eyes.

"Oh man, what happened?" Desmurose asked as his vision was still blurry.

"Are we dead?" Allucio said curiously.

"No, we are alive," Wyler spoke. "I don't know how, but we are."

Master Renzfly sat up slowly, everyone else did as well. They all grabbed hold of their heads, trying to stop the ringing in their ears.

"That was not the outcome that I was expecting in that battle," Nuncio said as he slowly regained his energy.

"Where's Menzuo?" Amiata asked as she looked around the dead planet.

"He's over there," Wyler pointed to his right. He was sitting by a bunch of crushed rocks with Solar.

They all stood and walked over to him. "Menzuo, are you okay?" Scoop asked curiously.

He didn't raise his head. "I'm sorry, guys. I have failed you and the universe."

Solar jumped in as well. "She was too powerful. We weren't even close to having a chance against her. I am sorry as well," he looked into the sky. "Now, we are stuck on Legerdamien."

Master Renzfly stood over them. "Stop having pity for yourselves," he said sternly. "No one said that this was going to be easy. So what if we have a little setback. We can't let this stop us."

Menzuo stood to his feet and looked up to the sky. "A little setback? Look where we are, Master! While you guys were still unconscious, Solar and I tried to find a way out of here. There is no way out! We're stuck on this dead planet."

"Enough!" Master Renzfly shouted, "I have never taught you to give up, and I am not going to start now. You are the universal protector, and you have to believe that. Menzuo, Solar, look at me!" They both looked him directly in his eyes. He continued. "Look around, we are all here with you. We believe in you. So what if we lost a battle, we still have to finish this war. You have to believe that nothing and I mean nothing is going to stop you from saving the universe. Not even this. Now pick your heads up and be strong!"

Menzuo took a deep breath and looked at all of his friends. He let out a heavy sigh. "Thank you, guys, for having faith in me. I know if I get another chance at her, I'll take her out."

"Now that's the Menzuo that I know," Desmurose said happily.

"Phew, I thought you were punking out on us," Allucio jumped in jokingly.

Solar took a deep breath and looked around. "Well, it looks like we'll be here for a while, so let's get moving. We need to find a way out of here and fast," he instructed.

They all nodded and started to walk through the dead planet very cautiously, hoping to quickly find an exit.

Chapter 6

The Final Judgment

The panel of Universal Life was called back to meet once again in the board room, they were all seated and waiting for King Zenshuo to play the days past. Ambassador Naos took his seat, hoping that he was awaiting good news about his home planet. Everyone talked to each other very worriedly about the fate of Earth. It pained Ambassador Naos to hear the fearful thoughts of the panel.

King Zenshuo slammed his gavel down three times and called the meeting to order. "Quiet, please!" he said sternly. "I now call to order the judgment set upon planet Earth," King Eojtaf and Naos sat patiently as King Zenshuo continued. "As you all know, our team of protectors has been sent to Earth to restore order. We will now watch the universal screen to see if they have been successful."

Naos situated himself in his chair and looked over to King Eojtaf, knowing that his daughter had accompanied the rest of the warriors on their journey. No words were said, but they both knew what the other was thinking. The screen flashed and came on quickly. They all watched closely as the picture entered Earth, showing all of the carnage and destruction. Naos clenched his teeth as he looked at the painful sights. He could feel Earth's energy being sucked right out of it. "This is not good at all. I pray that Menzuo and the others have destroyed her," he said to himself as he continued to watch the screen.

King Linka from planet Kedurion put his hand on Naos' shoulder, trying to ease his fears. "Do not worry, my friend. Menzuo and the others will be fine," he said, trying his best to cheer him up.

Naos sighed, then nodded. He could only hope that what he was about to see was promising.

As the minutes changed to hours, everyone could see Menzuo, and the others were locked in combat with Queen Eaziah and the Pirate Drones. Everyone leaned forward in their seats as the battle waged on. They watched the warriors fight off the millions of Drones one after another, efficiently and successfully. The Drones were falling and quickly disappearing at the hands of the Solar Warriors. Confidence was building inside of Naos and the others on the panel. The Solar Warriors were in complete control.

Suddenly, the picture froze on Menzuo and Queen Eaziah as they floated high in the sky. Their battle was just beginning. The sight of Menzuo pounding on that dreaded beast made the entire panel cheer with joy. King Zenshuo had to quiet the room. He did not want anyone to get too excited over the sights of this slight victory. Everyone settled back into their seats and watched happily.

King Linka leaned over with a huge smile. "I told you, my friend, everything would be just fine. You see, Prince Menzuo is doing it, he's really doing it!"

Just as Ambassador Naos started to smile, he heard a burst of sinister laughter coming from the dust cloud that Menzuo created from pounding the Pirate Queen into the ground. At that moment, everyone noticed Menzuo flying higher into the sky. Just as the laughter grew louder, they saw a flash of light flying directly into the fading dust and directly through Queen Eaziah, splitting her in half. The panel saw Menzuo standing on the ground and Eaziah's severed body floating helplessly in the sky

"He did it!" the King from Thoratuls yelled. "Menzuo is victorious!"

Everyone started to cheer happily as they thought that Queen Eaziah's reign of terror had ended.

Ambassador Naos stood confidently and looked at King Zenshuo with a smile. He nodded back to him with pride. He was proud of his son and of the Solar Warriors.

As the universal panel continued to cheer, King Eojtaf noticed a smile fall across Queen Eaziah's face. He quickly raised his hands. "Everyone quiet down! The battle isn't over!"

The room fell silent. Everyone sat back, all except Ambassador Naos. At that moment, a purple fog leaked out from both parts of the Queen's separated body. The mist quickly regenerated into two new Queens. Naos fell back into his chair in shock. "How can this be?" he remarked as the fear resurfaced in his heart.

Before anyone could say another word, both Queens went on their attack upon Menzuo and the Solar Warriors. The universal panel watched helplessly as the warriors got the life beat out of them. "No, no, no! Not my planet! What's going to happen to my world?

King Zenshuo didn't budge the entire time as he watched his son continuously get slammed into the last standing buildings. As the panel continued to watch the screen, they noticed Queen Eaziah slamming Menzuo's limp body into Springfield's City Hall.

"I can't believe this. How can this be happening?" Naos said to himself. The other warriors were gathered and placed next to Menzuo at the steps of the building.

Naos couldn't watch anymore as the Queens stood over the warriors and grabbed hold of each other's hands. In an instant, the young warriors were covered with a pink fog. As their bodies were no longer visible on the screen, they all heard a massive explosion. King Zenshuo, Eojtaf, and Naos knew that the Solar Warriors were defeated. Everyone listened as the Pirate Drones cheered in victory.

After a few seconds, King Zenshuo made the universal screen disappear. The room was dead silent. He stood from his seat, angrily, but refused to show any part of his frustration to the panel. He looked around the room and yelled loudly so that everyone could hear. "To the universal panel of life, the judgment upon Earth...has been set. Due to the outcome of the battle that we have just witnessed, I have no choice but to destroy planet Earth. I must relocate the energy of all good and evil to somewhere safer within our universe," he looked over to Naos. "I am sorry, my friend, but this has to be done. We have no choice," he raised the gavel high above his head and slammed it once onto the table as hard as he could.

The sound of the hammer made Ambassador Naos' heart sink to his feet. Naos lowered his head painfully. "This couldn't have happened. This has to be a bad dream. It has to be a very...bad...dream."

"Load the Huro bomb immediately! We will launch it in five hours. Within twelve hours of the launch, planet Earth will no longer reside in the inner realm," King Zenshuo slammed his gavel down one more time to end the meeting.

Mumbles rolled through the crowd as everyone exited the room. King Eojtaf sat next to Naos, both were filled with sorrow. "My poor little girl, she was so young, how could that beast do that to her? My beautiful little girl."

Naos was still in shock. He slowly turned to King Eojtaf with a depressed look. "If my planet goes, then I go!"

King Eojtaf quickly lifted his head with tear-filled eyes. "What are you planning to do?"

"I'm going to save my wife and my kids. I am going to kill as many of those Drones as I possibly can, and maybe, somehow, I'll kill those beastly Queens," Naos stood to his feet. "But if I don't defeat her, I will die honorably."

Eojtaf stood next to him. "Whatever you do, put me down for it as well. I have lost the most precious item in my life, so I owe her just as much as I owe you."

King Zenshuo walked out of the board room with his head hanging low.

"Follow me!" Naos said quickly. He and Eojtaf ran out of the board room, down the hall after the King.

King Zenshuo stopped as he heard both of them running behind him. He quickly turned and looked at their faces, knowing precisely what they wanted to do. "Naos, Eojtaf, I cannot allow you both to risk your lives because of that outcome," he looked over to King Eojtaf. "Our children knew what could happen. They fought valiantly, but unfortunately, they were unsuccessful. We must move on and let the universe repair itself. We must stand strong and protect all other existing life."

"How could you say that? How could you be so cold?" King Eojtaf said with shock. "That beast killed your son as well. Those Pirates have taken two of your children. You know she will come directly after you if she finds the energy of all good and evil. We have to do something."

"Plus," Naos jumped in, "my family is still on Earth. I have to get them off."

King Zenshuo lowered his head. "I know the pain that you are feeling is great. I, as well, am deeply hurt," he looked up to the ceiling as the pain of losing another son rushed through his body. "You are right Eojtaf, I have lost two of my sons at the hands of these Pirate Warriors," Zenshuo paused then looked back into Eojtaf's eyes, "But I must look at the bigger picture. I have the entire universe to look after. I cannot put you two in harm's way. We have to take care of universal business."

"But what about my family? Are they supposed to just die with Earth?" Naos asked as he jumped in King Zenshuo's face.

Zenshuo lifted his head and could see the pain ripping through their souls. He let out a deep sigh. "I cannot hold off the Huro bomb, but you may go and save your family, Naos. I will be overseeing you two. Once you have recovered your family, you and King Eojtaf must leave quickly. These are my orders. Do you understand?"

With a stern look on his face, Naos answered. "I understand."

"I understand as well," Eojtaf responded.

"Good, hurry back, my friends, and please be careful. I do not want to mourn more than I have to," Zenshuo quickly turned and started to walk down the hall again. "Remember," he shouted, "I will be observing you two on the universal screen.

"Thank you, King Zenshuo, I know that this was a hard decision for you to make, but you have made the right one," King Eojtaf responded

"I do hope so, my friends, just don't do anything crazy. Return here immediately after you recover your family, Naos," King Zenshuo said as he opened a door. He exited the hallway, leaving both of them standing there.

Ambassador Naos stood next to his friend. "Let's get going. We don't have any more time to waste," he said in a severe tone.

"I'm right behind you," King Eojtaf responded. They both walked down the hallway and out of the castle. Naos and Eojtaf knew that their lives were in grave danger as they got onto the spaceship.

As the ship floated in the sky, King Zenshuo watched them through a window and prayed for their safe return. "I know what you both are going to do," he said to himself, "You two are great warriors, and I will never let anyone question that. I pray that you both will return, but I know that you probably won't. May the souls of the past warriors be with you."

The spaceship disappeared into the clouds and blasted off towards the inner realm.

Chapter 7

Souls of Legerdamien Attack

Although Scoop and Wyler returned most of everyone's energy, they were all still too weak to fly. The Solar Warriors walked cautiously through the dead planet as they breathed in the moist night air. Everything was gray and dreary as if the life was completely sucked out of it. They knew that nothing ever lived peacefully here.

"I wonder if King Zenshuo is going to destroy Earth," Allucio said curiously as they moved along.

"Probably," Desmurose answered, "If they watched what happened to us, you better believe he will."

"But we're still alive," Allucio responded.

"We know that, but he doesn't," Amiata jumped in.

"That is right," Master Renzfly answered with a smirk. "We are dead to everyone, including Queen Eaziah."

"So, what is so good about that? We're still stuck on this dead planet," Menzuo said in a stern voice as he kicked a rock along the path.

"I understand that, but being dead to them, is what we need for those Queens to think. If we can get off of this planet, we can battle them again, and this time, we will not fail." Master Renzfly said confidently.

Menzuo quickly stopped walking, making everyone else stop as well. "But Master Renzfly, those Queens are way too powerful for me to defeat. I failed badly."

"I know you did, Menzuo, but I know you have learned from that battle, and will be much more prepared to face her the next time," Master Renzfly walked over to him. "Now, did you give up when you faced Hydrosion?"

"No," Menzuo replied.

"Did you give up against Morbid?"

"No."

"What's different now? So what if she's stronger than you. I know that if you have confidence in yourself, you and Solar will find her weakness and destroy her. Just remember, my Prince, no warrior can win every battle, and only great warriors can win the wars."

Those words made Menzuo feel much more confident about himself. "You're right, Master Renzfly. Man, you always know exactly what to say."

"Menzuo," Nuncio jumped in, "You know that we are behind you wherever you go."

"I know, and I appreciate that. I couldn't ask for better friends," Menzuo nodded and continued to walk again.

As they journeyed on, they noticed a cave ahead. "Let's rest in there before we run into one of these evil ghosts on this planet," Scoop said quickly. "I know that we don't have enough energy to fight in any type of battle at this point."

"You're right," Solar agreed. "It will feel good to get off of our feet for a while. Maybe we can figure something out while we rest," they all headed up to the cave and quickly entered.

As the Solar Warriors rested, Menzuo, Allucio, and Desmurose were all thinking about their parents as they were still in the ship that was resting on the moon. Allucio chuckled as he thought about their parents.

"What's so funny?" Menzuo asked.

"Your parents," Allucio answered as he was still chuckling. "I wonder what their reaction was when they woke up on the moon."

Menzuo and Desmurose thought about it, and they both started to laugh. They were happy that their parents were safe, but they could see the comedy in all of it. "I know my dad probably had a heart attack," Menzuo said with a smile. "Now that would be a sight to see."

"Yeah, but our parents will have to explain everything to them, Desmurose responded with a similar smirk. "It's going to be fun trying to make them believe that they are not the only planet that is populated in this universe."

"I can't wait to see them again," Menzuo said with a sigh.

"You will, my Prince," Solar answered, "I can guarantee it."

Princess Amiata sighed heavily as well. "I hope my dad doesn't do anything crazy. I hope he's not headed to Earth. If he saw what happened to us, I know he would."

"You do have a great father, Princess Amiata," Master Renzfly jumped in. "I know with the thought of you gone, Ambassador Naos and your father will head to Earth." He walked over to her. "You know, your father and I have fought side by side on many occasions. He even saved my life once."

Amiata perked up. "He did?"

Everyone listened in as Master Renzfly continued. "Yes, I was just about to meet my maker by the hands of one evil Pirate Warrior when your dad pulled me out of the way of his blast. We were all in an epic battle to save planet Vascora. We won that war, and your dad was given the prestigious Yardanian medal of courage. King Eojtaf put his life at risk to save many people during that war," Renzfly smiled with pride. "Your father was one of the best warriors that came from a neighboring planet that was trained under the Yardanian fighting style," he looked back into Amiata's eyes. "Not being from planet Yardania made his medal more prestigious. So don't worry, my Princess, your dad knows how to handle himself in battle."

Amiata was filled with pride after hearing his words. "Wow, my dad, was that good?"

"Even better than you could ever imagine," Master Renzfly stated.

After hearing that story, the Solar Warriors were now fully energized and ready to get on with their search for getting out of Legerdamien.

As they stretched their bodies, they all heard noises coming from deep inside the cave. "Who is in my cave?"

Wyler stood quickly. "Did you hear that?"

"Who is in my cave?" the angry voice spoke out again.

They all stood cautiously. "Who is there?" Menzuo yelled back.

"Who is in my cave?" the voice shouted louder.

Everyone stood ready to protect themselves from whatever was calling out to them. "I...I don't like this," Scoop said as his heart pounded in his chest.

Solar tried his best to focus on any type of energy that would be inside of the cave, but there was none. "I don't know who or what it may be. We must check it out before it finds us first."

Master Renzfly nodded as he walked with his guard up. He moved deeper into the darkness of the cave. "Everyone, stay close."

They all followed behind him as he moved deeper into the darkness. The voice continued to yell out. "Who is in my cave?"

As everyone continued to walk closer to the sound of the voice, they all noticed a dim light in the distance. "Who's in my cave?" the mysterious voice continued to shout out.

The Solar Warriors paused as they looked at the light growing brighter in the distance. "It is Menzuo and the Solar Warriors," he yelled back.

In an instant, the light disappeared. "What happened?" Allucio shouted. "Did we scare it?"

Before anyone could say another word, the ground started to move beneath their feet. The bright shining light instantly reappeared, almost blinding them. As they covered their eyes, the Solar Warriors were sucked deep into the cave.

After a few seconds, the young warriors were able to clear their vision. They all noticed that they were standing in a small room that had candles hanging from the walls. "Where are we?" Scoop asked.

"I don't know, but I think we are safe," Solar replied as they all looked around. "I don't sense any danger."

The room within the cave was quiet. It gave off a feeling of peace as the team stood in the center. There was no damp smell of death lingering, and there was absolutely no darkness. The Solar Warriors began to relax.

A few moments later, the mysterious voice spoke out again. "So you're the live souls stuck on this disgusting planet? What a shame."

"Who are you?" Menzuo said as the figure walked from around the corner.

"I am Chackup. I was an elite guard on Yardania many, many years before any of you were born.

Master Renzfly stepped forward. "I've heard stories about you. You were an excellent warrior. You helped train with Master Kane."

"That is correct," Chackup responded. "Unfortunately, my powers weren't strong enough to save him when he became evil. Even when he killed me, I was proud of Kane," Chackup said with a half-smile. He sat in a chair in one of the corners of the room directly under a lit candle. "Please sit. Rest yourselves."

They all sat down, keeping their eyes on him. "How can we get out of here?" Menzuo questioned.

"I can't help you with that. You have to ask 'the Master' for that," he responded.

"The Master?" Allucio asked.

"Master Kane himself. He's the only one who can open Legerdemain's portal, leading out of this planet. Although, you'd better run into the right Kane. If you happen to meet his evil twin, you'll be stuck here for life. It's a fifty-fifty chance of running into either one of them."

Menzuo stood. "Where can we find the right Master Kane?"

"Young warrior, Prince Menzuo," Chackup said as he leaned forward. "I have heard many stories about you. I always wondered if we were ever going to see another universal protector, and here he is. It is an honor to meet you."

"It is nice to meet you too, but excuse me for my lack of patience, where can we find Master Kane?" Menzuo answered.

"Do not apologize," Chackup responded. "I understand why you all are in such a rush. If you are lucky, you can find 'the Master' over by the warrior's cemetery. There, you will find the tombstones of all dead warriors. You might run into some trouble on the way. The evil souls of Legerdamien would love to make sure that you all never make it off of this plane."

As the group took in everything that Chackup said, a very slick and small creature crawled into the room, over to Menzuo without anyone noticing.

"How do we get there," Master Renzfly asked.

"Just walk out of the cave and head west. It's just a few minutes from here."

Menzuo could feel the blue diamond moving from his neck. He quickly looked down and noticed a little gray hand toying with it. "Hey!" Menzuo shouted as he jumped back. He looked at the yellow-eyed creature as it smiled back. The bottom half of his body looked like horse legs. The top part of his body was covered with a bluish-gray fur, and his head was slick. Its eyes were the most significant part of its upper body. "What the hell is that? It was trying to steal my necklace."

Chackup clapped his hands, calling the creature over. "I am sorry, Menzuo," he said in a calm tone. The beast sauntered over to him. Everyone stood but cautiously kept their eyes on Chackup as he went on. "He is not a thief. His name is Neon. He's a moon jumper. Many years ago, he somehow made his way to this planet. When I found him, he was hiding from several of the evil Pirate souls. I saved him from being taken into their side of the planet. Ever since that day in the valley, he's been by my side."

Neon crawled on all fours over to the Solar Warriors. He stood on his back legs and smiled. "Neon says hello to the Solar Warriors. Neon has heard many great things about the Solar Warriors. Neon says he wants to help the Solar Warriors," he looked over to Menzuo. "Neon says he's sorry for scaring Menzuo.

Neon says that the diamond on the necklace reminds him of his moon home. Neon says he misses his moon home."

Desmurose looked over to Chackup. "He speaks a lot?"

"Oh yes, I taught him a long time ago. He's pretty good at it too."

Menzuo walked over. "It's okay Neon, I'm just a little jumpy. I hope I didn't scare you."

"Neon says he is not scared. Neon says he knows Menzuo wouldn't hurt him," Neon answered.

Master Renzfly spoke out again. "Chackup, will you allow Neon to help us find the warriors graveyard?"

"Yes, my little friend is very cunning and knows his way around this planet. He spends most of his time outside. He has never been seen nor even chased by a Pirate Ghost since his first day here. Moon jumpers are tough to detect."

Master Renzfly rubbed his chin. "To tell you the truth, this is the first time I have ever seen a moon jumper up close. I thought they weren't friendly creatures?"

"They usually aren't, but when you get to know one, they become very loyal," Chackup responded.

"Neon says, let me lead you to 'the Him.' Neon knows where 'the Him' is."

Menzuo nodded. "We would be honored if you showed us the way," everyone got ready to leave the cave. "Thank you, Chackup."

"Just take care of Neon, he likes you guys a lot, and oh, don't worry, I'll be seeing you real soon," he said to Menzuo with a sinister smirk.

They all watched Chackup chuckle as they walked out of the cave.

"What did he mean by that Master Renzfly?" Menzuo asked.

"I don't know. Let's just get to Master Kane and get out of here," They all jumped down from the cave. They followed closely behind Neon down a path leading west to the warrior's cemetery.

~Menzuo~

A few minutes passed as they walked down between two massive black mountains. As they continued on, they started to hear noises bouncing off the mountain walls. "Neon says to be cautious."

"Yeah, you never know what will jump out at us," Amiata agreed.

Before anyone could react, a voice yelled out. "You are absolutely right about that."

Neon stood straight up on his hind legs. "Neon says uh oh! Neon says this is not good!"

116

Everyone froze as they looked at Neon, spinning in circles, trying to find a way out of the mountains. "Neon says uh oh! Neon says, uh oh! Neon says the evils are here! Neon says he must hide. Neon says he leaves the Solar Warriors to fight."

"What?" Scoop shouted angrily. "You're leaving us right now? In this open valley! What type of guide are you?"

Neon ran over to a crack in the mountain wall. "Neon says a living guide. Neon says good luck, Solar Warriors," he slid into the crack and quickly disappeared.

"I knew it! I knew it!" Allucio said, "Chackup set us up. We should have never trusted him and Neon."

"I think it's too late to be mad at them now," Nuncio answered.

A cold breeze quickly blew past them. "Get ready, I think we're about to have a little fun," Desmurose said.

Everyone noticed several shadows passing over their heads.

"This will not be any type of fun for you living warriors," one of the dark figures said as it stood on the top of the mountain. "We are going to kill you and make sure your souls are stuck on this planet forever!"

Allucio stepped forward. "Show yourselves then! We're ready for whatever you think you're going to do!"

"Not a problem!" the voice shouted back. In an instant, seven ghosts flew down from the top of the mountains and blocked the pathway. They lined up side by side and looked at the Solar Warriors angrily.

"Power up, we have some business to take care of!" Master Renzfly shouted.

A few moments later, everyone was ready to battle.

"Well, well, well. What a pleasant surprise!" one of the ghosts said. It stepped forward. "Good old Master Renzfly; I have some unfinished business with you."

Menzuo looked at Master Renzfly with a smile. "You know this ghost?"

"I know them all. That is Fyrdraca. Do you remember the story I told you in the cave?" everyone nodded as he went on. "That was the Pirate that King Eojtaf saved me from."

"Oh, I get it; he's mad at you, huh?" Amiata said with a chuckle.

"Of course, that's why I'll take care of him," Master Renzfly responded.

"Who are the others, Master Renzfly?"

"To Fyrdraca's left, you have Gravlax, Ibex, and Pyrocet. To his right, you have Maduro, Doblo, and Protiest. They were some of the evilest Pirate Warriors to have ever come into the universe."

"I guess we can punish them a little more for what they did in the outer realm," Menzuo said.

"I'm happy to see that you have your fighting spirit back, my Prince," Master Renzfly responded.

"Me too," Menzuo responded confidently. "Okay, you ghosts. Get ready to suffer more pain than you ever did alive! Aaah!" Menzuo quickly charged towards them, the other warriors followed his lead.

"You want it...you got it!" all of the ghosts charged as well. The death world battle had begun.

Neon peeked through the crack of the mountain. "Neon says he doesn't want to miss this. Neon says he likes a good fight. Neon says wishes he had some moon rocks to eat."

Chapter 8
Warrior's Fight for Earth

As Menzuo and the Solar Warriors were battling for their lives on the dead planet of Legerdamien, Ambassador Naos and King Eojtaf were making their way towards Earth. "I hope that my family is still safe," Naos said in a worried tone.

"I'm sure that they are my friend. You have hidden them well," Eojtaf responded, hoping to make him feel a little more at ease.

Naos shook his head. "Those poor people on my planet, I know they are suffering on Excervo. It must be the scariest place that anyone has ever set foot on."

Eojtaf placed his hand onto Naos' shoulder. "We'll get them back, Naos. Somehow, we will save them."

Naos took a deep breath and let it out slowly. As he did, they could finally see planet Earth in the distance. Continuing to fly closer, the two warriors could feel the two Queens' enormous energy. "Oh my goodness, that was what Menzuo and the Solar Warriors were up against? Her energy is unbelievable!" Naos said. His eyes widened with the fear that rose within him.

"How can something or someone be that strong?" Eojtaf questioned.

They both looked at each other, knowing the battle that they were about to enter could possibly be their last.

Naos refocused his mind on the thick pink cloud as they got closer. "We're about to enter Earth's atmosphere. We have to lower our energy so that we cannot be detected," he continued to fly the spaceship closer to the planet.

"No problem," Eojtaf responded.

In an instant, they both lowered their energy and made the ship invisible. Naos put the engine on silent float and slowly descended into the embattled world.

As they cautiously broke through the pink cloud, slowly lowering the ship onto Earth, Eojtaf and Naos watched swarms of Pirate Drones flying around, guarding the area against intruders. Naos weaved in and out of the crowd and headed for the Atlantic Ocean. He was disgusted by the sights that his eyes had to endure. "I can't believe these Drones. They have destroyed my home. I'm going to make them pay for everything that they have done."

"Yes, we will, Naos. We will make them pay, my friend," King Eojtaf added.

After a few quick maneuvers through the surrounding drones, the ship was directly over the center of the Atlantic Ocean. "We're here," Naos made the ship hover in place. He opened the door cautiously, looking around to see if any drones were nearby. He was hoping that they would not be detected this early. "Stay close to me. We are about to enter my hidden temple," Naos jumped out of the ship and into the water.

Eojtaf nodded, following him out. As they dropped deep into the ocean, Eojtaf noticed something extraordinary. "Why aren't we wet? We are in the water, am I correct?"

"Yes, we are. I have used a unique technique to keep us dry. At this exact spot, there is a hidden passageway that leads to the royal temple. Without my powers to separate the water, no one else can get down here."

Eojtaf looked around as they floated to the ocean floor. "That's a nice trick," he answered. The King was very impressed by the sights that he was able to see on planet Earth. Many curious sea animals observed them as they passed.

They finally reached the ocean floor and stood in front of a wall of water. Naos moved his hand slowly from left to right. In an instant, a large passageway opened for them. "The temple is just ahead. We have to hurry. I know we don't have much time."

"I'm right behind you," Eojtaf answered as they walked the path.

As they reached the temple, Naos and Eojtaf stood in front of two solid golden doors. Naos knocked three times. As he did, an enormous blue whale appeared from above the temple. The whale swam closer and spoke with a deep voice. "I am Sir, the protector of the Ambassador's temple. You must address yourself properly before you are allowed to enter Earth's temple of life."

Naos stepped forward. "I am Ambassador Naos of Earth. I am with King Eojtaf of planet Bralose. Sir, we are here to rescue my family."

Sir moved one of his more enormous eyes so that he was looking directly at both of them. He studied the warriors for a few seconds. "Ambassador Naos? It has been a very, very long time."

"I know, my friend," Naos said in a sad voice. "There haven't been any emergencies on Earth in a long while. I didn't have to use the temple for safety."

"I understand," Sir answered. "Although, I hear we are now in grave danger. Are those words that I speak true?"

Naos dropped his head and let out a sigh. "Unfortunately, they are, Sir. The Pirate Queen Eaziah has defeated Prince Menzuo and the Solar Warriors. She has taken a huge portion of our upper world. At this moment, there is no stopping her. Because of this fatal outcome, King Zenshuo was forced to send the Huro bomb to destroy Earth. Within the day, there will be no future for our home."

Sir swam above Naos and Eojtaf and looked into the sky. "What is he doing?" Eojtaf asked.

"I think he's trying to feel what is going on in the upper world. He'll be just a minute."

"Hmm, this is very strange, very strange, indeed!" Sir spoke loudly.

"What is it, Sir?" Naos asked.

Sir took in a deep breath and let it out. "I can sense a good life up there. Yes! Yes! The universal protector and his friends are alive!"

Naos' and Eojtaf's eyes widened. "But...but how? We watched the two Queens destroy them. It's just not possible. You must be mistaken," Naos stated emphatically.

"On the contrary, Ambassador Naos, it is very possible," Sir swam back down to them. "The warriors are alive, but they are no longer on planet Earth. They seem to have been placed on a very cold and what seems to be, a very dead planet far, far away from here."

Eojtaf jumped in quickly. "It sounds like they are on Legerdamien, the warrior's death world. That is very strange, how did they end up there...and alive?"

"Strange things can happen when you possess the blue diamond," Sir stated.

"The blue diamond?" Naos questioned. "I thought that was a myth."

"No myth, my friend, Prince Menzuo, found the mysterious energy that was left for him by the last universal protector. He truly possesses its energy now."

"I didn't recognize that he had the blue diamond while we spoke on planet Yardania. I was so wrapped up thinking about the safety of our home. This is unbelievable," Naos said as he looked up into the sky. "That is truly unbelievable."

"Are they okay?" Eojtaf asked, wondering about his little girl.

Sir looked back into the sky. He was quiet for a moment as he refocused on the Solar Warrior's energy. "It appears that they are locked in a fierce battle with the evil ghosts of Excervo. The outcome is very unclear from so far away," the doors opened to the temple as Sir swam away. "Ambassador Naos, King Eojtaf, although I think that failure is imenent, there is hope. Earth still has a chance," he disappeared back over the temple.

"They are still alive!" Eojtaf said excitedly. "We can hold off the Queens and the Drones until they return. Somehow in some way, they will make it off of Legerdamien and return to Earth. Then they can destroy these disgusting beasts."

Naos nodded confidently. "I was planning on battling her to the death anyway, but now that there is hope, I will be glad to sacrifice myself."

Eojtaf grabbed Naos by the arm and held him tightly. "I am right with you, my friend. I had the same intentions as you upon our arrival. King Zenshuo knew what we were going to do. So, if you go into battle, I will go with you."

"Then let's get my family out of here. I can't wait to battle these beasts," Naos said confidently. They both walked into the temple confidently, ready to protect Earth.

They walked to the back of the castle. Naos opened the living room doors, noticing his kids playing. They turned their heads, and upon the sight of their father, their eyes lit up. "Daddy! Daddy!" Korra and Talen yelled as they ran over to him. They quickly jumped up and gave him a big hug.

"My children, I've missed you," Naos said lovingly.

As his kids were placed back onto the ground, Korra noticed a man standing behind her father. "Who is that daddy?"

Naos turned to introduce him. "This is King Eojtaf of planet Bralose. He's a good friend of mine."

"Hello, King Eojtaf," Talen said. Naos rubbed his full head of hair. "It is nice to meet you."

"It is nice to meet you, my young Prince and Princess," Eojtaf said with a smile.

They both bowed politely. Naos kissed both of his children on the head. Korra and Talen ran out to the back room. "Mommy! Mommy! Daddy's here!"

"Beautiful kids," Eojtaf said, "Now I know why you had to return."

As he said that, the doors opened, and Anisa stepped through. Out of respect for mother Earth, King Eojtaf kneeled and bowed as she walked forward. "Please stand, King Eojtaf. There is no need for the formalities."

"With all due respect, I must do so, as I am a guest on your home planet," Eojtaf replied. He stood back up. As he focused on Anisa's face, his mouth dropped. He noticed that she was aging quickly as planet Earth was losing its energy.

Anisa walked closer to her husband. "You travel with a man of great respect."

Tears quickly filled Naos' eyes as he looked at his wife. Because of what the Queens have done to Earth, mother Earth Anisa's image had changed drastically. She was now showing her actual age. Fully wrinkled, and very frail. Naos stroked her gray hair gently. "Honey, I am so sorry that this has happened to you," he hugged her gently so that he wouldn't hurt her. As he was finally able to relax, he slowly pulled away. "I must get you and the kids off of the planet. Earth is in danger of being destroyed."

"As you can see, my dear," Anisa said, looking down at herself. "Much damage has already been done to our planet. Those ladies up there have really destroyed the structure of our home. There isn't much holding her together. If she dies, I pass with her."

Naos started to grind his teeth as he was getting angrier by the minute. "I promise you, my dear, those Queens will surely pay for what they have done," his blood was boiling.

King Eojtaf stepped forward as he could see his friend about to break. "My lady, it is time that we get you and the children to safety. You will head to Yardania, where my wife will meet you."

Mother Earth stood very confused. "What about Menzuo and the others?"

"They lost the first battle, but they are okay. They were sent to Legerdamien. We are hoping that in some way, they will return to fight for Earth again."

Anisa looked deep into Eojtaf and Naos' eyes as something shook her fragile bones. "What are you two planning to do?"

Naos lowered his head and sighed. "We have to hold the Queens off until our young warriors return. It is our only chance to try to save you and our planet. If we don't, the Queens will completely drain Earth of all of its energy. We cannot sit and watch you, as well as this planet, die. We don't have much time as we are facing the wrath of the Huro bomb as well.

Anisa dropped her head. "Oh, my, I know you must protect Earth, but please be careful. I do not want to lose you, my love."

Naos picked her head up slowly by the chin, making her look him in the eyes again. "I will do my best to be safe, but you know the nature of my job. If I must die for our planet, then I must die."

Tears streamed down Anisa's face as she caressed his. She looked over to Eojtaf. "You be careful as well. I would hate for Queen Vanera to lose you."

Eojtaf bowed. "I will be as careful as I can, Mother Earth."

Naos gave her one last hug then pulled away slowly. "Now honey, get the kids together and get to the emergency ship. In about fifteen minutes, launch off this planet and head for Yardania. King Eojtaf and I will be there when we are done."

Anisa started to cry even harder. "Please come back to me," she said in a very shaky voice.

"Go now, my dear," Naos said as the tears fell from his eyes.

Anisa nodded. She walked to the back room and closed the door.

Eojtaf put a hand on Naos' shoulder. "Never forget that we are fighting for the survival of the universe as well."

Naos picked his head up and wiped his face. "I know. Let me get ready. I'll be back in one moment." Naos took a deep breath and walked over to his closet.

As the Ambassador opened the door, Eojtaf noticed a long black and silver outlined trench coat. "That must be the famous battle trench, huh?"

Naos quickly slipped it on. "Yes, it is. I can't remember when I last wore this. I never thought that I would have to take it out again."

Eojtaf smiled. "We'll make sure that you get some good use out of it."

Naos slid his fingers through his dreadlocks. He looked over to the table and opened the drawer slowly. Ambassador Naos grabbed a long razor and held onto it tightly. He reached to the back of his head and grabbed his locks. Extending them out as far as he could as he closed his eyes. With one quick movement, Naos cut them all off. He turned around and looked to King Eojtaf with a solemn expression. Letting the dreadlocks dropped to the floor, he nodded. "Are you ready, my friend?"

King Eojtaf closed his eyes and held out his hands, making them glow. He slowly rubbed them together. As he did, a full set of body armor appeared around him. Opening his eyes, King Eojtaf cracked his neck and smiled. "Now, I'm ready."

Naos nodded with respect and confidently walked out of the temple with friend by his side.

As soon as the readied warriors reached the outside of the temple, Naos took one last look at it then waved his hand from right to left. The doors closed, and the temple slowly disappeared. He looked over to Eojtaf. "Let's get it done!" they both powered up and shot out towards the top of the ocean.

Chapter 9

Revenge of the Pirate Ghosts

"Mega body attack!" Menzuo shouted as Doblo charged.

As soon as Menzuo's bombs were close, Doblo made his body hollow. The attack flew right through him. "That won't work on me! There is no chance of blowing me up," he laughed as he made his body whole again. "I'm already dead! Aah!"

Menzuo smiled as he floated backward. "I wasn't trying to blow you up. I was just letting you see what was about to hit you."

Before Doblo could react, the three fireballs hit him directly in the middle of his back.

His body picked up speed flying out of control as he got closer to the mighty Prince. Menzuo paused as his enemy was just a few feet away. "How did you do that?" Doblo yelled frantically.

"Easy!" Menzuo replied. He balled his fist tightly as Doblo's out of control body flew closer. "Eat this!" Menzuo violently punched Doblo, stopping his body's forward motion.

Menzuo's fist was deeply imprinted into Doblo's face. Without hesitation, Menzuo continued to pound the ghost's body rapidly, not allowing him to recover. He drove Doblo back, quickly thrusting him right into one of the mountain walls. Over and over, the Prince continued his attack until the mountain crumbled around them.

As the wall continued to fall, Menzuo shouted. "Wild rage!" a green light shined through the cracks, brightening the entire valley.

A massive explosion occurred, shooting boulders from the mountain high into the dark sky.

As the black dust filled the air, Menzuo flew out of the cloud and floated into the sky. He watched as the rest of the mountain fell on top of Doblo. "That was too easy," Solar said jokingly.

Menzuo smiled confidently. "He wasn't a smart Pirate. He was overly aggressive, so I used that against him."

"I must say, you are getting smarter with every battle," Solar answered as he brightened the blue diamond.

"I have a great partner," Menzuo answered as he noticed Doblo's soul disappearing. He looked around to see how his friends were handling their ghosts.

Master Renzfly and Fyrdraca were locked in a furious battle just a few hundred yards from everyone. The two were fighting at a blinding pace. Punch after punch and kick after kick was thrown with no regard for one another. Neon peeked through his hiding place and noticed that Menzuo was victorious and the others were still fighting. "Neon says that he likes the Solar Warriors. Neon says the stories are true about them," he ducked back into the crack, hoping not to be seen.

As the flashes from each punch and kick brightened the dark sky, Master Renzfly was preparing to make a drastic change in the battle. "Nothing is going to stop me from destroying you this time, Renzfly!" Fyrdraca yelled as he continued to swing ferociously.

"Well then," Master Renzfly answered. He continued to block Fyrdraca's attack with his right hand as he lowered his left. "Eat this!" he shouted, quickly pointed his hand at Fyrdraca's mouth. "Solid freeze!" an ice bomb flew from his palm, directly into Fyrdraca's mouth and down his throat.

Fyrdraca grabbed his neck as his eyes bulged. His throat froze. "Gasp...gasp...gasp!" the ice ball slowly froze the inside of his body. "What did you do...to me?" Fyrdraca said with his last bit of breath.

"I made sure that I left your soul in pain," Master Renzfly responded. "Goodbye, for now!" He kicked Fyrdraca violently in the chest.

Master Renzfly's attack sent Fyrdraca's frozen body straight towards the ground.

"You will pay for this!" Fyrdraca yelled angrily.

The ghost was fully encased in ice. Fydraca's body exploded into millions of pieces as it hit the ground. The ice crystals quickly melted and seeped into the cracks on the death world path. Master Renzfly floated down as Menzuo made his way over to him with a shocked look on his face.

"What was that?" Menzuo said in amazement.

Master Renzfly cracked a little smile as he watched Fyrdraca's frozen body continue to melt away. "One of my most fierce attacks, my Prince."

"Shoot, I want to know how to do that now," Menzuo responded.

A loud bang grabbed both of their attention. Master Renzfly and Menzuo quickly looked back into the sky only to see their friends still locked in deadly battles.

"How are the others doing?" Master Renzfly asked as he relaxed.

Menzuo spotted them in different parts of the sky. "They are all still battling those Pirate Ghosts up there. We should go help them!" Menzuo said anxiously.

Master Renzfly grabbed him by the shoulder. "No! They have to fight their own battles. It will make them much stronger if they are to win against these Pirates. This is a true test of the Solar Warriors."

Menzuo sighed and tried to relax. Deep down, he knew that Master Renzfly was right. They watched the others battle the Pirate Ghosts high in the sky as they awaited the outcome of each individual battle.

King Scoop and Wyler were fighting off Gravlax with great force. Princess Amiata was deep in combat with Protiest. Allucio had his hands full with Maduro. Desmurose and Ibex were lighting up the sky with each punch thrown, and Nuncio was handling Pyrocet with everything that he could give.

The clouds flashed like lightning, and the ground rumbled as the thunderous blows echoed through the planet. Scoop and Wyler jumped from mountain to mountain as Gravlax threw huge boulders towards them. "C'mon! You can do better than that!" Wyler yelled. Another smoking boulder exploded on the hill that they jumped from.

"Don't run from me! Let me crush you, you puny little men!" Gravlax yelled angrily.

Scoop quickly turned around just after he jumped from another mountain top. The smile left his face and was replaced with anger. "What did you call me?" Scoop asked. He and Wyler paused as they floated next to a mountain wall.

Gravlax paused as well, generating another smoking boulder in the palm of his hands. "Oh, I must have struck a chord with you two. I called you and that twerp, puny! What are you going to do about it?"

"Oh, that's what I thought you said," Scoop responded, looking to Wyler then nodded confidently. He quickly clapped his hands. "Hecto gammit!" at that moment, Wyler started to grow. He grew until he was ten times his average size. He was now twice the size of Gravlax. "You will pay for that!" Wyler's muscles bulged from every part of his body as he floated in front of Gravlax. "Who's puny now?"

"Ah! Ah! Ah! Unbelievable!" Gravlax could barely speak. He was in complete shock as he looked up at Wyler's face. Shaking uncontrollably, he dropped his smoking boulder. "How…how…how did you get so big?"

Wyler smiled sinisterly. "Magic!"

Wyler took hold of Gravlax by the face and started to pound on his chest. Over and over, he continued to punish the Pirate Ghost.

Scoop rubbed the fingers of his right hand together, instantly creating a handful of dust in his palm. He floated over to Wyler and smiled. "It is time."

Wyler stopped the beating, finding that Gravlax was very weak from the attack. He let go of his face and let his limp body fall. The rock ghost was dazed and almost drained of all his energy.

Scoop blew the dust into Gravlax's face and floated back. He quickly yelled. "Reata rock!"

As the dust-covered his face, Gravlax tried his best to fan it away. "What is this?"

"These are my rock eaters! Say goodbye!" Millions of magical insects appeared all over his body. Their enormous mouths held rows of sharp teeth. The beetle shaped insects were ravenous and had a good meal on hand.

"No! I will see you again, and I will be ready!" Gravlax shouted just as the rock eaters destroyed his body. As soon as Gravlax had been dispensed, the little insects faded back into the magical dust.

Wyler shrank back to his average size. He and Scoop floated down to the ground next to Menzuo and Master Renzfly. As they landed, Menzuo could see that Scoop was still angry. "What's the matter now? You both defeated him."

"Yeah, but I hate it when people call me puny!" Scoop said as he tried to relax.

Menzuo chuckled. "But you have a big heart, and that's all that matters."

Master Renzfly kept his eyes on the sky as the other battles waged on. After a few seconds, Menzuo, Scoop, and Wyler looked up as well. A thunderous blow shook the ground.

"Princess Amiata's battle with Protiest will decide our fate," Master Renzfly said in a severe tone.

Menzuo looked at him. "Why is that?" he asked.

"Because Protiest has the most strength out of all the Ghosts, he's been here the longest, so his powers are more developed than the others. The balance of power lies within that battle."

"And we can't help her, right?" Menzuo stated quickly.

Master Renzfly shook his head as he kept his eyes on Princess Amiata. Menzuo looked up as well and focused on her battle.

Each punch and kick that Amiata and Protiest threw, echoed through the dead planet. The lightning-fast strikes brightened the sky as if a storm was on the rise. Allucio, Desmurose, and Nuncio were still entrenched in a battle with the other remaining ghosts.

Protiest and Amiata floated back from each other. "Ha, ha, ha, ha! You will never beat me. Young lady, I am the key to you all getting out of this planet. If you do not defeat me, you will be the cause of your friends having to live here forever."

Amiata smiled. "Well then, you have picked the wrong Princess to mess with. I'm not the dainty little girl who lives under her parents' reign. I am a warrior, and I will prove that to you."

"Are you serious?" Protiest answered with a chuckle. "You are not any type of warrior. I have been toying with you, letting you build your confidence in the meanwhile, but since you think you are worthy of being called a warrior, I'll be glad to prove you wrong."

"Here's your chance. Go ahead and try!" Amiata shouted back.

Protiest's body started to glow. "C'mon little girl!" in an instant, they both charged towards each other with violent force.

"Here we go!" Master Renzfly said. "This is it!"

The collision caused an enormous explosion. A bright white light filled the sky. As it faded, Amiata and Protiest continued their deep hand to hand combat. They punched and kicked each other over and over at a blinding pace. They battled tirelessly as their bodies slowly floated towards the ground.

Not Amiata nor Protiest would give in as they both landed about twenty feet from Menzuo and the others. "Come on, Amiata!" Menzuo shouted, trying his best to encourage her. Master Renzfly, Scoop, and Wyler didn't budge one inch as they all waited for someone to emerge victoriously.

Neon poked his head through the crack, trying to watch their tireless battle. As he looked into the sky, a flash brightened the area.

"Aah!" Princess Amiata screamed in pain.

The light quickly disappeared as Amiata's body flew past Menzuo and the others, directly into the side of the mountain that was behind them.

"It is done," Master Renzfly yelled. "Amiata has lost."

"No! No!" Menzuo screamed. "How? Why?" he barked.

Protiest started to laugh. "I told that little girl that she was no warrior. She should have given up earlier. What a waste of my energy."

Menzuo quickly powered up. "I'll make you pay for that! She was my friend!"

"Neon says, Princess Amiata lives on!" he shouted.

A rumbling came from behind the group, making Menzuo pause just before he charged into battle.

The rocks from the mountain exploded. Princess Amiata stood confidently as the dust cleared. Menzuo turned around and noticed her standing with a white glow around her. "I am not done yet!" she screamed.

Master Renzfly stood very shocked. "But how? I could have sworn that her energy was depleted? This is unreal for a Bralokian Warrior."

Scoop chuckled as he stepped back. "The Princess looks fine and a bit angry, to me."

Menzuo smiled as he began to relax. "Yes, she is! She is pissed."

In a flash, Princess Amiata charged towards Protiest and pushed him back.

"Oh, no!" Neon screamed as he quickly jumped out of the crack in the mountain.

"You lose!" Amiata shouted as she shoved Protiest right into the mountain wall that was directly behind him. She didn't waste any time, not hesitating to release her vicious attack. She built all of her energy into her hands and screamed. "Fury strike!" a huge orange ball flew from her hands, directly at the mountain as Protiest tried to make his way out of the rubble.

"What?"

The attack slammed right into his chest and planted him back into the hole. The rest of the mountain fell on top of him.

Amiata quickly flew over his body as he was half-conscious and still on his back. As Protiest sat up, she pointed her palms towards him. "This is for my father and for thinking that I'm some weak little Princess! Fury strike!" one large orange and green flaming ball flew from her hands, directly towards Protiest.

Protiest shook his head as he was finally able to open his eyes. He slowly looked up into the bright light. "Noo!" he screamed.

The attack closed in far too fast, giving him no chance to move out of its way. The bomb exploded into his body, making his ghostly shell disappear.

"She did it! She did it!" Menzuo screamed with joy.

Amiata slowly floated to the ground. She was weak from the battle but still had enough energy to stand tall. As she landed, the rest of the ghosts that Allucio, Desmurose, and Nuncio were battling started to disappear.

"What happened?" Allucio shouted as Maduro faded.

As Ibex charged towards Desmurose, he quickly disappeared as he swung at Desmurose's body.

"Wait…what? Where did he go?" Desmurose questioned as he looked around curiously.

The same thing happened to Pyrocet as Nuncio filled his hands with his final attack. As he disappeared, Nuncio relaxed. "It is over." He took a deep breath then floated to the ground.

Allucio, Desmurose, and Nuncio returned to where the others were standing. "Great job, Princess Amiata, you have broken the link of the ghosts. We depended on you, and I, for one, am very impressed with your power. You are going to be a great warrior," Master Renzfly said.

"Thanks, but I almost blew that battle," she answered. "I don't know what came over me. I felt like all of the past Bralokian Warriors were giving me the strength to continue to fight."

Without regard to Amiata's conversation, Allucio quickly jumped in. "Um, can anyone tell me what just happened?" he said curiously. "I was just about to finish that ghost off, but he just disappeared. Was he that afraid to lose?"

"No, Allucio, Princess Amiata destroyed the most powerful ghost and broke their link to fight us," Wyler responded.

"So that's why they disappeared," Desmurose said. "Are they gone forever?"

Master Renzfly shook his head. "No, they are still here on this planet. Their energy is regenerating somewhere else. These ghosts are stuck on this planet for all eternity. They cannot die, and their power will return to them shortly."

"Will they be back any time soon?" Scoop asked.

"I do not know, but if we do not get off of this planet, you can definitely expect them to be back and they will be much stronger," Master Renzfly stated.

"We have to find a way out of here quick," Menzuo responded. "That was a great test, but I don't think we need another one."

Neon slowly crawled out from another hiding place. "Neon says, great job to the Solar Warriors. Neon says the stories are true. Neon says he is very impressed."

Allucio quickly tried to grab him by the throat but was suddenly stopped by the others. "You little punk, you almost got us killed. I'm going to wring your little neck when I get a hold of you!"

Neon backed up against the mountain wall. "Neon says, he is sorry! Neon says that he had to make sure that all of you were the true Solar Warriors! Neon says that he did not mean any harm by what has happened. Neon says he is a true believer now. Neon says that he knows that you are the true Solar Warriors."

Menzuo quickly walked over to the trembling moon jumper. "Why did you set us up? I thought you were going to help us."

Neon hunched over as he crawled towards Menzuo, trembling. "Neon says he is going to help Menzuo and the Solar Warriors. Neon says he was following Chackup's directions. Neon says he was told to test Menzuo and the Solar Warriors to make sure they were ready to meet 'the Him.' Neon says he was doing what he was told."

Menzuo took in a deep breath then let it out slowly. "Are there any more tests?"

Neon shook his head. "Neon says no more tests. Neon says the Solar Warriors have proven themselves. Neon says, 'the Him' is ready to see Menzuo and the Solar Warriors."

"What does he mean by that?" Nuncio asked.

Master Renzfly looked up above one of the mountains. "I think what is up there is what Neon is talking about."

A dark shadow appeared on top of the mountain. The Solar Warriors felt an immense amount of energy rising. Another warrior was looking down at them as they stood on the path leading to the warriors' cemetery.

"Wow! Menzuo shouted. "Whatever it is, it is strong, time to power up, guys!"

Everyone followed Menzuo's lead and powered up. A red glow came from the face of the shadow where its eyes should have been. The warrior quickly jumped from the mountain and landed just a few feet from the Solar Warriors. "Neon says this is going to be good. Neon says no hiding from this one."

They all took a step back and readied themselves for another battle. The Solar Warriors were very tense as they waited for the mysterious warrior to move.

Chapter 10
Fighting for Earths' Survival

Naos and Eojtaf emerged from the water, and flew towards land. Operating at a lightning pace, they made the water build-up behind them, creating a massive tsunami. Flying at that speed, it wasn't long before they were right over Springfield, Massachusetts.

As they closed in on the city, they could see the downtown area burning in the distance. Eojtaf looked at Naos with a smirk as the Pirate Drones flew just below. "Would you like to do the honors?"

Naos nodded and yelled. "To all Pirate Drones, you are no longer welcome on this planet! Leave now or die!"

All of the Drones below stopped and looked up, noticing Naos and Eojtaf floating higher in the sky. "Come and get a piece of us!" Eojtaf shouted as he waited for their attack.

"Raaack!" a Pirate Drone screamed, alerting the other Drones that were situated all over the city.

"Here we go!" Naos shouted, "Thanks again for staying by my side."

A flood of Drones closed in on them from every direction. "No problem, my friend. I wouldn't want it any other way," Eojtaf responded as they floated back to back. "Let's make them pay! Fury strike!"

"Blade attack!" Naos shouted. He threw two silver disks at the charging Drones that were flying towards him.

Both Naos and Eojtaf's attacks blew away hundreds of Drones, but the flood grew larger with every passing second.

The Drones continued to scream loudly as they circled the two warriors.

Without any hesitation, Naos and Eojtaf punched and kicked each Drone that tried to fight back. They were quickly knocking them out of the sky, making their bodies smash into the ground.

Each of the warrior's blows landed violently against the swarm of Drones.

"Come On! I know you skunks can do better than this!" Eojtaf yelled violently as he continued to fight them off.

"Blade attack!" Naos yelled.

"Fury strike!" Eojtaf shouted.

Both warriors continued blowing away as many Drones as they could. Their furious battle made the Drones that were near, back off just a bit. Breathing heavily from the amount of energy spent,

Naos and Eojtaf circled, staying back to back as they kept their eyes on Excervo's evil minions.

"We're not giving up!" Naos shouted.

"You'll have to do better than that to get rid of us," Eojtaf followed.

A soft rumble in the distance grew stronger. Both Warriors quickly looked up, noticing a shadow covering them. Eojtaf and Naos started to feel the Drones getting stronger.

Naos took a deep breath. "Here, we go again!"

The sky was quickly covered with a black wave of Drones, slowly darkening the sky. With the sight of them closing in from above, Naos finally broke away from Eojtaf's side. "It's time to battle alone, my friend!" Naos shouted. "Good luck!" He darting higher into the sky towards the black cloud of evil.

Eojtaf quickly realized what he was doing. "Go, Naos! These Drones down here are all mine!" He generated all of his energy into the palm of his hands. "Fury Strike!"

Eojtaf's attack stopped many of the Drones that were trying to chase his friend.

As the Ambassador closed in on the falling Drones that were above him, he quickly put his hands into the pockets of his battle trench coat and fanned it out as wide as it could go. At that moment, the edges of the coat turned razor-sharp. The gleaming silver edges blew in the wind, making them move like silk.

A flood of Drones that once floated in front of him were cut into pieces. The separated Pirates slowly fell past Eojtaf, down to the ground. As their bodies crashed into the decimated city below, they disappeared into the black ooze.

All of the Drones that surrounded the two warriors paused for a second as they watched their sliced brothers disappear. Angry as ever, they finally redirected their attention to Naos and Eojtaf. Both Warriors could see that they made the Drones much more Furious.

"Roar! Roar!" the Drones screamed with rage. Once again, they charged into battle.

Now that Naos and Eojtaf figured out how to get rid of those dreadful minions, they knew the battle turned in their favor.

"I'm happy to have gotten your full attention!" Eojtaf said with a smile.

"Oh, you want some more?" Naos shouted.

Over and over, the Ambassador and the King of Bralose continued to cut down the attacking Drones.

Eojtaf raised his right hand high above his head. "Lightening rod, form!" he shouted. An electric staff quickly appeared in his hand. He spun it over his head, making the wind furiously push the Drones away from him, creating more space for him to move in the sky. As he lowered the staff, he pointed and waved them all in, still with a sinister smirk on his face.

"Roar! Roar! Roar!" the drones screamed as they charged towards Eojtaf with their mouths wide open. Swinging their sharp claws at his body, trying to kill him with each swipe.

"Static shock!" Eojtaf Shouted. He instantly electrified each one of the charging Drones that he made contact with. Their bodies disintegrated into the black ooze and disappeared into thin air.

As Naos and Eojtaf continued to fight off the massive swarm, the streets of downtown Springfield were covered entirely with the ooze from the bodies of the defeated Drones. With each precise movement, Eojtaf and Naos sliced through and electrified every minion that got in their way, not letting them get the upper hand.

"C'mon! You can do better than that!" Naos screamed as he sliced open fifty more Drones with one strike.

"I'll kill all of you if I have to!" Eojtaf shouted angrily as he spun his staff behind his back, electrifying a fleet of Drones.

At that moment, a loud noise shot out from over the ocean. It was the spaceship carrying Mother Earth Anisa, and the children.

Naos heard the blast and looked back as he fought off the Drones. "They're going to make it!" he said happily as he continued in his battle.

The space ship flew closer to the sky, Naos noticed the two Queens appearing just a few feet from the aircraft. Both of them raised their hands, making a pink glow form around them.

"Goodbye, my lovelies. What a shame, Mother Earth and her lovely children will die by the hands of the new Queens of Earth," the red Queen said softly.

Mother Earth looked out of the window with tears in her eyes as she noticed Naos in the distance. Anisa looked to both Queens, shaking her head with complete disgust for what they had done to her home planet. "You will pay for this one day," she said softly.

"Mommy?" Korra and Talen said together as they hugged her tightly, burying their heads into her lap.

"Noo!" Naos screamed frantically. "Leave them alone!" he generated an abundant amount of energy into the center of his body and let it go. "Blade attack!" Naos shouted as loud as he could.

The blast shook the entire city. The energy flew from every part of his body and blew away thousands of the surrounding Drones, making a clear path for him to get to the exiting ship.

"Sensing Densor!" Naos shouted, instantly disappearing, leaving the Drones floating in the sky, looking for him.

"Bye, bye, and lots of kisses!" the blue Queen said then blew a kiss to Anisa, releasing her vicious attack.

The red Queen did the same, and they both watched the two pink balls of fire fly towards the ship.

"Noo!" Naos yelled as he reappeared in between the ship and the Queens' attacks. The Ambassador opened his coat and caught the energy bombs. He quickly closed it, making both bombs explode onto his chest.

The sound was muffled, but the damage clearly showed on Naos' face. From the expression of pain, the Queens knew that Naos was severely damaged. Pink smoke seeped out of the lining of his battle trench coat.

The Drones that were fightinh King Eojtaf quickly stopped and moved away, leaving an opening to the sky for him to see Naos floating helplessly in front of the two Queens. Eojtaf immediately noticed the spaceship exiting the planet. "Good job, my friend. I'm on my way," he said then took off towards the helpless Ambassador.

Naos' eyes were glazed over as the blue Queen slowly flew closer towards him. She ran her fingers through his short hair and caressed his head with a sinister smile flowing across her face. "The valiant Ambassador Naos, how stupid of you to take on our energy bombs. What were you thinking, my lovely? You might have saved your family for now, but they will all die when we take over the universe for our husband, Lord Fetid."

The red Queen felt Eojtaf's energy getting closer. "Ooh! Excuse me, my dear, I have some company coming to visit," she responded to the blue Queen.

The blue Queen turned and batted her eyes lovingly to her sister. "You know what to do with him. Take your time. I know he'll love the pain."

The red Queen flew towards Eojtaf, ready to block his way. "This will be so beautiful," she said with a smirk.

As Eojtaf closed in on her, he made his energy level rise to its highest peak. "Just what I've been waiting for, Take this! Mega fury strike!" one large orange and green flame flew towards her.

The red Queen paused and floated in place. She opened her mouth as wide as she could and swallowed Eojtaf's energy bomb. "Mmm! That was very sweet of you! Another, please."

Rage built through Eojtaf's body. "Aah!" he screamed angrily as he closed in.

The King swung violently at the red Queen's face, making each punch connect with brute force. The sky flashed from each violent blow.

As Naos heard the red Queens moan from Eojtaf's attack, he slowly lifted his head with a smile on his face. "It sounds like we have a fighting chance!"

The blue Queen looked confused as she heard the battled Ambassador speaking. Just before she could respond, Naos opened his jacket and let the two energy bombs fly straight out into her face. "Take this!" Naos shouted. He swung the bladed edges of his jacket towards the Queen.

"Aah!" the blue Queen screamed as her hand was cut off from her body. It was stuck in Naos' hair as she tried to back away.

Looking at the stunned Queen, he noticed something sparkling on her face. Naos quickly reached for it and grabbed hold of the pearl that was in the middle of her forehead. He tried his best to pull it off. "I hope this works!"

"What are you doing? Noo!" the blue Queen continued to scream in pain.

As Naos tried to pull the pearl from her face, he noticed that the dismembered hand that was stuck in his hair started to turn to stone. He looked at the Queen as she struggled to make him let go. "That's it! It's the pearl! The pearl is your weakness!"

"Let go, you don't know what you are doing to me, aah!" the blue Queen pleaded.

"I know exactly what I am doing! Take this!" he tightened his grip and pulled away violently, ripping the pearl from her forehead.

"Eeyaah!" the blue Queen screamed in absolute pain as she balled her fist.

Without letting Naos make another move, the blue Queen punched him in the stomach, knocking the wind completely out of his body.

She continued to punch Naos as her face started to turn to stone. His grip around the pearl began to loosen.

Naos finally succumbed to her last punch.

The Ambassadors hand went limp, making him finally release the pearl. The blue Queen caught it as it fell from his grasp. She quickly reconnected it to her face. "You little fool! How dare you do that to my beautiful face?" The blue Queen felt the left side of her face. It was now covered in solid stone. "I don't care if you found my weakness. You will never get a chance to do that again!"

Naos held tightly to his stomach as he tried to regain his breath. "I...I might not...but I know who will."

The blue Queen's face turned sour. "No one will ever kill us! We are the most beautiful and most powerful beings in this universe," she lifted his head once again. Her eyes turned bright pink. "Let me show you how strong we really are. Pink rush!" she yelled, making a colossal energy bomb fly towards his body.

Naos could only put his hands up to try to block her attack. The blast was too strong and blew Naos back. His helpless body quickly shot past Eojtaf, back into downtown Springfield, like lightening.

The ground exploded as he hit it. "Naos!" Eojtaf screamed as he stopped punching the red Queen.

"Bad move, honey!" the red Queen said softly, "That was feeling great too. You should have never stopped."

The red Queen punched Eojtaf right in his face, making his eyes blur. "The supreme, King Eojtaf, from planet Bralose, you really thought that you were accomplishing something, didn't you. I was just waiting for my sister to plant Ambassador Naos into the ground so that I could do the same with you." Her eyes brightened with the same pink flames. "So take this! Pink rush!" she screamed, making a massive pink energy ball blast Eojtaf from over the water and back into Springfield as well.

Just as fast, Eojtaf's body landed right next to Naos.

All of the Drones surrounded them as they were lying on their backs, trying to open their eyes. The Drones growled and snapped their teeth, ready to tear the warriors apart. As they were just inches from grabbing Eojtaf and Naos, the two Queens quickly appeared above them.

The Drones felt their enormous energy and slowly backed away. "I think it's time that we had a little more fun while or children," the blue Queen said.

"That sounds lovely to me. I have a wonderful taste for pain, deep in my belly!" the red Queen responded.

"Drones! Search for the energy of all good and evil, and destroy any life that you may find in the wake. Go now!" the blue Queen shouted.

All of the Drones quickly dispersed from the area in search of the all-mighty energy.

Naos tried his best to stand to his feet with his eyes still blurred. "You can do what you want with us, but I promise that you will pay for all of the destruction that you two have caused!"

"Tisk, tisk, tisk! The poor Ambassador is delusional. He thinks that he's going to kill us off," the red Queen said as she put her hands on her hips. "I must say, what a warrior's spirit you have."

Eojtaf finally stood to his feet as well. He shook his head, trying to clear his vision. "He is right, you ugly excuses for Queens. You will pay. It will be a wonderful day to see you both suffer."

"Ha, ha, ha! What funny men you are," the red Queen stopped laughing and turned her face up. "I don't think you understand that your lives will be over soon, and so will the existence of this wretched planet."

Naos lifted his head confidently as he stood with pride. "Well then, why don't you both just enjoy yourselves, you nasty freaks!"

Both of the Queens were now very angry at the two warriors' responses. Their horns started to glow violently. The wind quickly picked up around them.

"The both of you will suffer a long and painful death. Your life means nothing to us!" the blue Queen shouted.

"It is time that you both feel our wrath!" the red Queen followed.

"It is time to die! Eeyaah!" they both shouted.

The Queens charged in.

Both Naos and Eojtaf barely had enough strength left in their bodies. "We must hold on, Eojtaf! For the Solar Warriors! For Menzuo!" Naos shouted as they both held their arms out, welcoming the Queens' attack.

"We will!" Eojtaf screamed confidently.

Both of the Queens drove Naos and Eojtaf's bodies deep into the ground. Everything that was left standing in downtown Springfield quickly crumbled from the Earth-shattering quake.

The two Queens didn't waste any time. They picked up the two warriors from out of the deep holes and threw them high into the sky. The Queens disappeared then reappeared just above Naos and Eojtaf's limp bodies.

"This will be very exciting!" the red Queen said to her other half as they got closer.

The Queens knocked the two helpless warriors back down towards the ground like missiles.

The Pirate Queens continued to disappear and reappear in different areas in the sky as they continued to pummel the two warriors as if they were human yo-yos. Faster and harder, they moved with their attacks.

With every solid blow that was delivered, the Queens could hear the sound of Naos and Eojtaf's bones breaking within their bodies.

With one simultaneous last kick in the small of the warrior's backs, the two Queens shot Eojtaf and Naos high into the sky. They smiled at each other, then quickly rushed up to their enemies.

Naos and Eojtaf's helpless bodies broke through the clouds. Their bodies paused as they were now able to see out of the planet, directly into space. The valiant warriors started the uncontrolled decent back toward the ground.

The Queens floated next to them, given the warriors kisses on their cheeks. "Pink rush!" they shouted.

The two energy bombs drove the warriors speeding towards Earth. They were falling directly back to the holes that they were once in. The cloud from the impact filled the sky. The crater sunk for miles, deep towards Earth's core. As the dust cleared, a rush of water shot out of the ground, high into the sky. The downtown area was beginning to flood.

Both the red and blue Queen floated above the holes, waiting to see if Naos and Eojtaf had the will to survive.

After a few minutes, the water spouts settled. Both Queens noticed that Eojtaf and Naos had pulled themselves out of the holes. With the little energy that they had left within their bodies, they tried their best to stand.

"I can't believe this. These warriors have high thresholds for pain, honey. Now I am truly impressed. I must apologize for thinking that they were weak," the blue Queen said.

"Yes, I know, my dear, but this outcome will make our playtime more enjoyable," the red Queen responded. "I could have sworn that they would give up by now. In some strange way, it makes me proud to torture these two."

Naos stood to his feet but was very wobbly. He looked up with one eye open. "Bring it on!" he yelled, as blood dripped from his mouth.

"That was nothing!" Eojtaf jumped in.

Both semiconscious warriors started to laugh. "Ha, ha, ha! That was a feeble effort you two gave us. We expected more."

The Queens' faces quickly turned. "We'll see who will get the last laugh!" the blue Queen shouted.

Within seconds, the two Queens shot down towards the ground. Naos looked into the sky. "Please…hurry, Prince Menzuo! I do not know how much longer we can last!"

Chapter 11

Master Kane's Offer

As the mysterious warrior stood in front of them, Master Renzfly spoke softly. "Put your guard down, everyone, we are safe."

The warrior standing confidently in front of them wore very tattered clothes. His face was defined with war wounds, and his body was etched perfectly with muscles as if he was chiseled from stone. A smile fell upon his face. "Master Renzfly is correct, you can all put your hands down. You are safe."

Everyone dropped their guard as Menzuo stepped forward. Neon followed closely behind. "Neon says speak clearly. Neon says, don't be afraid. Neon says it is the Him."

Menzuo looked the warrior right in his eyes. "Are you Master Kane?"

"Yes, I am," he said confidently as he looked down at the blue diamond that was placed upon Menzuo's necklace. "I see you have recovered the blue diamond."

Menzuo looked down at it. He put his hand over it. "This was yours, right?"

"Yes, it was. As my spirit began to grow evil, I knew of only one way to bottle some of my good energy to save it for the next universal protector. That is if we were ever to have another such protector."

Menzuo sighed. "It has come in handy, but I still do not know how to release all of its power. King Scoop has taught me how to unlock it in the short amount of time that he had to train me, but I can sense there is more to it," Menzuo said.

"You are correct, young Prince. I believe that the blue diamond has already given someone close to you a gift."

"Yes, it has," Menzuo answered. In an instant, the blue diamond started to glow, and out floated Solar.

Master Kane chuckled. "I see that you have regained your body, young warrior Prince."

Solar looked at his hands then back up to Master Kane. "Yes, thank you for this gift. I have to tell you, it still hasn't hit me that I have my body back. It was a refreshing feeling to be able to walk and fly again, but I'm happy that I can still help Prince Menzuo through his battles."

Master Kane nodded. "I am happy that you are joined with Menzuo throughout his life. That bond will never break, but some other changes may occur soon."

Menzuo looked very confused. "Like what?"

"That cannot be revealed to you as of yet. Understand this, you are very much capable of reaching a level of supremacy that I, as the universal protector, could have never reached. Because of your extraordinary strength that is now combined with the energy from the blue diamond, you, Prince Menzuo, will one day control the fate of the entire universe."

Menzuo nodded, indicating that he understood. "What about the prophecy of the universal protector? I was told that it is possible that what happened to you can easily happen to me."

Master Kane sighed. "That prophecy is just that, a prophecy. Only you can control the outcome of your life. Every decision that you make leads you down a different path," he started to pace back and forth. "Being the first universal protector, I have been given many gifts for saving the universe. The way that I left was something very extraordinary that no one has ever experienced. Because I sacrificed myself for the betterment of the universe, I was given the gift to foresee two possible future outcomes of the outside world," Master Kane looked back to Menzuo and Solar. "I can honestly tell you that you must stay focused on each and every battle that you are in. Some decisions that you will have to make will be tough, but you must make them for the betterment of the universe."

Neon crawled from behind Menzuo. "Neon says Menzuo and the others will make only the wise decisions, 'the Him.' Neon says they are the best warriors he has ever seen. Neon says he is impressed by the young age of the warriors, too."

Menzuo looked down. "Thank you, Neon, for the compliment, but we are still mad that you set us up."

Master Kane stepped forward and stroked Neon's head. "Do not blame the moon jumper. He is loyal to his guardian and listens to whatever he is told. The test that you were put through was set up by me. I had to see if you all were truly ready to protect the outside world."

"So how did we do? Do you think we are ready?" Desmurose asked.

Master Kane looked at the rest of the warriors with a straight face. "Almost," he said as he walked back over to Neon. "There is always room for improvement. Luckily you have a great trainer by your side. If Master Renzfly wasn't with you, I'd be very wary of the outcome of your fate."

Master Renzfly bowed. "Thank you for the compliment, Master Kane. It's a great honor to hear that coming from you."

"My friend, it is an honor to know a great warrior like you. You are an elite breed of warrior and a fine one at that. Take pride in training these young warriors. I can tell you, if you all stick together, the universe will speak your names for centuries."

"That is very nice to hear," Princess Amiata said softly, "But what about the war that we are currently in with the Queens on planet Earth?"

"You will return soon enough to your fate. You all will either prosper or fail miserably," Master Kane turned and walked back over to the warriors. He stood right in front of Amiata. "May I?" he said softly.

"Yes," Amiata answered, then lowered her head.

Kane put his hand on top of her head and closed his eyes. "What is he doing?" Wyler asked.

Neon made his way over to the group. "Neon says Master Kane is reading her energy. Neon says Master Kane is reading the two outcomes of her fate. Neon says he likes 'the Him's' powers."

A few seconds later, Master Kane released his grip from Amiata. He looked back into her eyes. "My young Princess warrior. Your life as a Solar Warrior will bring you great joy and a great deal of pain, but your journey as a warrior will be defined by one difficult decision. Make the decision that your heart will guide you to. If you do, balance can be restored when the time comes.

Amiata stood confused. "What do you mean by that Master Kane? I don't understand."

"You will in due time, my Princess. Just do me this favor, keep Nuncio close to your heart, and everything will fall into place."

Amiata stood confused but nodded with respect. She looked back at Nuncio. "I will."

Scoop walked over. "Master Kane, for many long years, I have heard great stories about you while I was stuck under the Naleezar's reign of terror. He knew everything about you. As a treat, instead of eating me, the Naleezar would tell me your life story. I have to say, what I have heard has sent chills down my spine."

Master Kane turned to Scoop. "The Naleezar was very accurate with his stories. There are many evil things that beast can do, but lying isn't one of them," Kane said with a half-smile. "I had a great time raising him, and as time went on, nature took its course, and he could no longer be controlled. I left him with the mission to protect the blue diamond until the right person came along. I bet he is agitated that Menzuo took it from him."

Menzuo smiled slightly. "Oh, he was, and he showed it by trying to eat me."

Master Kane walked back over to Menzuo. "I am sorry that you all do not have enough time to sit and talk with me. It has been a very long time since I spoke to someone who was not a ghost on this planet."

Menzuo looked up to the dark sky. "I wish that we could stay longer. I know you could probably help us prepare for this war, but there isn't enough time for that. We must get back to Earth as soon as we can to finish this. Will we be able to get off of this planet?" Menzuo asked.

Master Kane smirked. "Prince Menzuo, there is only one decision that you will have to make that will get you all off of this planet and back to Earth. It is your destiny to battle those Queens, but before I make my final request, I have to reveal something to you all," he said without blinking once. "Just like you, I am not dead. I reside on Legerdamien as the GateKeeper. I make sure that all of these dead warriors, good or evil, will never leave this planet. I am the only one who can open the passage that leads to the outer realm."

Solar stepped forward. "If that is so, then you can leave this planet at any time if you please?"

Master Kane shook his head. "It is not that easy. If I leave, then the evil Kane will be able to free himself from this planet as well. I control his fate just as much as I control my own. So my sacrifice is to always stay here, but enough about me," he said then looked back to Menzuo. "It is time for you to make a decision."

Menzuo's face went blank. "What is it?"

Master Kane put his hand on Menzuo's shoulder. "I will only allow you and your friends to leave this planet if you and Solar agree to my request."

Menzuo took a deep breath. "What decision is that?"

"If fate has it that you destroy the Queens, you and Solar must return to Legerdamien, alone." Everyone froze as he continued. "If you all succeed, the complexity of the universe will change drastically. Your duties as the Universal Protector, and as the Solar Warriors, will increase far beyond what any of you could ever imagine. Far beyond any obligation that I ever had to carry out. I want you, Menzuo, to agree to this so that I can train you, and Solar. If you agree, you will then understand the real usage of the power that I gave to you. You both will be better prepared to face Lord Fetid when the time comes."

Menzuo looked back at everyone as Master Renzfly spoke. "It is the only way, Menzuo," he said with a straight face. "You cannot turn down this offer."

Menzuo took a deep breath then let it out slowly. He turned back to Master Kane and nodded. "I agree to your terms. Now, can you show us the way out?"

Kane nodded. "I am proud of your courageous decision. I know that you are not aware of what you have gotten yourself into, but I promise both you and Solar will be better for it. When the time comes, I will call for you and Solar, but first, you must win this war. You must stay focused upon your return to battle."

"We understand, Master Kane," Solar answered.

Kane put his hand onto the blue diamond. "Here is a little gift for you to use when you face those beasts."

A blue glow covered Menzuo's body then quickly disappeared.

"Whoa! What was that?" Allucio shouted.

"You all will find out very soon," Master Kane responded.

"This is a great opportunity for Menzuo, Master Kane," Master Renzfly responded.

Kane nodded. "You, of all people, should understand the importance of this opportunity, Master Renzfly," he looked at everyone else. "One more thing, I need to show you this," Master Kane snapped his fingers, and in an instant, an oval screen popped up in front of them. A picture of Earth appeared, showing Ambassador Naos and King Eojtaf getting the beating of their lives by the two Queens.

"Daddy?" Amiata shouted as she watched her father get slammed into the ground.

"As you can see, Ambassador Naos and King Eojtaf are stalling the Queens from destroying that planet," the screen changed to several different areas around the city. "The Pirate Drones are searching for the energy of all 'good and evil.' Fortunately for you all, they will not succeed."

As the screen moved back to where Naos and Eojtaf were, everyone balled their fists in anger. "Are they going to die?" Nuncio asked.

"They may," Master Kane responded, "But these two warriors are doing this, knowing that you all are still alive. Even if they knew that you all were dead, they were ready to give their lives to save Earth. This is the true spirit of a warrior. To fight without fear, even if you know you cannot win."

Menzuo was now filled with rage and confidence as he watched Naos and Eojtaf continually getting pummeled by the Queens. He balled his fists as tight as he could. "We are ready, Master Kane. Please, open the gates."

Master Kane snapped his fingers and made the oval screen disappear. "I know you are, Prince Menzuo," he said, then pointed to the sky. As he did, the dark sky started to shine brightly in only one spot. "You must hurry. Naos and Eojtaf cannot hold the Queens off much longer. Their spirits are fading."

Menzuo nodded and quickly powered up.

Solar re-entered the stone. "Let's go! You heard Master Kane. We have to hurry!"

Just as everyone powered up, Scoop yelled out. "Wait, Menzuo!" he ran over to him. "I know that you can move through the universe at a much faster pace than all of us. I can feel the energy that Master Kane just gave you. Let me put you in the space

JUDGMENT SET UPON EARTH

jelly so that you can get to Earth and try to save Naos and Eojtaf. We will be right behind you. Our space jelly will only last for us to get to planet Bralose to pick up another spaceship. We will meet you and Solar very shortly."

Menzuo took a deep breath and nodded as the portal leading out of Legerdamien started to close. "You do not have that much time!" Master Kane yelled as he noticed some of the ghost making their way to the exit. "I can only hold it open for a few more seconds. The Pirate Ghosts are going to try to escape. Go now!"

In an instant, Scoop waved his hand over Menzuo and covered him with the space jelly. Menzuo quickly opened his eyes. "I will see you all very soon." The warrior Prince flew straight into the sky and shot out of Legerdamien like a bolt of lightning.

Let's go, everyone!" Master Renzfly shouted as Scoop covered the Solar Warriors in the Walonokian space jelly. They noticed a swarm of ghosts flying up to the closing portal.

The Solar Warriors all shot up towards the exit as well. "Thank you, Master Kane!" Nuncio shouted down to him as they quickly passed the ghosts.

"You are welcome. Make those Queens pay for what they have done to Earth," Kane shouted back as the Solar Warriors closed in on the portal.

Menzuo floated above the portal, just outside of it in outer space. He noticed everyone flying only a few feet away from the opening with the ghost's charging right behind. I'll see you all shortly, my friends!" he shouted. He looked down at the blue diamond as it started to shine. "It's time to get busy, Solar!"

Menzuo shot off at the speed of light, directly towards the inner realm, ready to finish what he started.

Just as the other warriors exited Legerdamien, the portal closed, blocking off the Pirate ghosts. "We made it!" Allucio yelled as they floated above the dark planet.

The Solar Warriors turned quickly and noticed the Huro bomb being released from Yardania. It was slowly heading towards Earth. "We must hurry back to Bralose and get another space ship."

Nuncio quickly shot off towards the planet as everyone followed closely behind. "If we grab my ship, we can be back on Earth in less than fifteen minutes. We can definitely beat the Huro bomb, but we will not have that much time."

"At the speed that it is traveling, I say that it looks like it will reach the planet within the next twelve hours," Master Renzfly said quickly. "There's no time to waste!"

"I hope that we can find a way to stop this bomb from destroying the Earth," Desmurose said with concern.

"We must handle the Queens and Pirate Drones first. Then we can focus on that issue," Master Renzfly said. "Let's go!"

They all looked off in the distance and noticed Menzuo's light stream as he headed towards Earth. "We'll see you soon, Menzuo," Desmurose said to himself.

As they flew towards planet Bralose, they noticed a bright being waving to them from the crest of Legerdamien.

"Goodbye, Neon?" Wyler said as he waved back.

"Goodbye," Desmurose added as he pointed to his left.

"I wonder if we'll ever see him again," Amiata said curiously.

"I don't know, but if we do, we may be living on Legerdamien full time," Scoop responded quickly.

"Where did he go?" Wyler said as he lost track of Neon as the clouds covered the planet again.

"He'll be fine. Those ghosts will never catch him. He seems to be fine on the Death World with Master Chackup."

"We can't worry about him now. We have far more important things to be concerned about," Master Renzfly said.

"We're almost there," Princess Amiata shouted as they closed in on planet Bralose.

"I can't wait to beat on those Drones. It's on this time! No holding back," Allucio said confidently.

Within a few minutes, Menzuo had already entered the inner realm and was less than two hundred miles from Earth. "Hold on, guys!" he said, thinking of Ambassador Naos and King Eojtaf. "I'm coming!" he shouted as he quickly passed Mars.

After a few hours of sleep, Steven and Krystal woke, a little calmer than the last time. Steven stretched and glanced out of the window of the space ship. "What's that flashing light out there?" he said curiously.

"I think it's a comet," Krystal followed.

"No," Michael Sr. said, "That is your son, Menzuo."

Steven's eyes widened as he watched the flash of light quickly pass the moon and dart right into the pink clouds that covered the planet. "You can't be serious."

"He's very serious," George added. "He's going to save our planet.

Krystal's heart started to beat faster than it ever had before. "Please be careful, honey."

Steven held tightly to his wife, trying to comfort her. They were very unsure about what was going on and really didn't want their son to get hurt.

It was quiet once again on the ship as everyone waited and hoped for a good outcome for their world.

~Menzuo~

Master Kane closed his eyes as he stood on the path leading to the warriors' cemetery. He watched the enraged warrior on his universal screen, fly into planet Earth. "Good luck, young Prince Menzuo. You will need it now more than ever."

Chapter 12

The Battle Continues

The two Queens continued to torture King Eojtaf and Ambassador Naos. They slammed the two warriors' helpless bodies into all of the burning debris that filled the city.

As they dropped Naos and Eojtaf near the Connecticut River, the two Queens hovered over their motionless bodies. "Tisk, tisk, tisk," the blue Queen said as she shook her head. "I believe they have finally given in to the torture."

The red Queen held her hand out just above them. "Mmm, yes, their energy is slowly fading. I do say that I am impressed by the way that they held on for so long."

The blue Queen sighed as they both floated down to Naos and Eojtaf's motionless bodies. The Pirate Drones that were in the area circled them as well. The Queens landed on the ground and continued to examine them. They were barely breathing as their eyes were closed entirely.

The blue Queen smiled. "I think it is time that we end our two lovely warrior's lives. I've had my fill of fun, how about you, my Queen?"

The red Queen nodded. "So have I. Let us send them off with the kiss of death."

"Rah, rah, rah, rah!" the Drones chanted as the Queens made their energy rise.

"This is it, Eojtaf," Naos mumbled. "Thank you for giving your life to save my planet."

"What are friends for?" Eojtaf responded as the Queens covered their bodies with a pink cloud.

"Rah, rah, rah, rah!" the Drones continued to chant as the Ambassador and King were completely covered. "Say hello to Prince Menzuo, and the rest of those disgusting Solar Warriors on Legerdamien for us!" the blue Queen shouted.

They both put their hands to their lips and blew soft kisses. "Resting blast!"

As they released their attacks, a silver flash flew directly into the pink cloud. "Sensing Densor!"

The pink cloud exploded. As the dust cleared, the Queens noticed that Ambassador Naos and King Eojtaf had disappeared. However, they could still sense their weak energy levels, accompanied by an enormous amount of power coming from somewhere nearby.

"What is that?" the blue Queen asked.

The red Queen closed her eyes and tried to focus on it. "I'm not sure. There is something familiar about that energy, though."

~Menzuo~

A few seconds later, Menzuo appeared with Ambassador Naos on one shoulder, and King Eojtaf on the other. They were on the top of a mountain in the distance, just a few miles away from the two Queens. Menzuo put them both down gently. "You two will be safe here. Just hold on a little longer."

As Naos slowly opened his eyes, he noticed a blurred figure standing above him. "M...Menzuo? I...is that you?"

"Yes, but please don't speak Ambassador. Your energy level is shallow. Try and hold on, Scoop and Wyler can revive both of you when they return to the planet."

King Eojtaf started to open his eyes as well, as he heard Menzuo's voice. "You...you have made it back. I knew you would make it," he said with a painful smile. "Those Queens really did a job on us!"

"I'll make them pay for that, I promise," Menzuo responded.

As he tried to sit up, Naos grabbed him by the arm. "The...the...the pearl," he said as his voice strained. "The pearl is the k...ey."

Menzuo looked at him very confused. "I don't understand."

"The...pearl..." before Naos could say another word, he passed out, and so did Eojtaf.

Menzuo sighed then finally stood. "Rest well, and thank you for risking your lives. This will not be forgotten," he turned and looked at the two floating Queens in the distance. "Time to rock and roll! Sensing Densor!"

As both Queens floated in the sky, they closed their eyes. The Queens could feel strange energy getting closer. They both sucked in an enormous amount of air in their lungs as their eyes widened. "Whatever it is, it will be here very soon!" the blue Queen said.

The Drones moved away in fear as the wind picked up. A few seconds later, Menzuo reappeared right in front of them. Both of the Queens' mouths dropped. "How is this possible? You are dead! We killed you!"

Menzuo crossed his arms as the blue diamond started to glow. "You never killed me. You just made me very angry."

The red Queen laughed. "That is so cute. The young warrior is mad at us."

"I love a confident fighter. You are the best ones to destroy," the blue Queen responded.

Menzuo tightened his fists. "There is no way that you two will ever destroy me! I am here to finish what I have started, and this time, I will not fail!"

"Well then," the red Queen said as she floated closer. "Why don't you show us how ready you are!"

"Alright! Haa!" Menzuo yelled as he powered up. In an instant, all of the Drones that circled them were blown back several hundred feet.

The red Queen backed away, shocked as ever. "My, my, my, you have gotten stronger in such a short while."

"I hope that you are impressed," Solar yelled from the blue diamond, as the other Drones started to back away.

The blue Queen smirked. "Oh, I see that you two are still together. How beautiful of a relationship that is. Too bad it won't last much longer."

"Don't get too happy," Solar responded as the blue diamond started to glow brighter. "We just might surprise you."

"Very well," the red Queen shouted. "I surely do hope so."

They both raised their hands and pointed them towards Menzuo. "Passion rush!"

As the blue and red flame flew towards the young warrior, he quickly crossed his arms and covered his chest.

Both flames hit his arms and exploded, leaving a substantial colorful cloud in the wake.

The two Queens felt an enormous amount of energy growing inside of the fog. They backed away slowly as it disappeared. As the cloud faded, there floated the rest of the Solar Warrior's, ready to help protect Earth.

"How is this possible?" the blue Queen yelled out. She was bewildered.

"Menzuo, we don't have much time!" Master Renzfly sputtered. "The Huro bomb is on its way."

"I understand," he responded. "Scoop and Wyler, I need you to regenerate Ambassador Naos and King Eojtaf's energy. They are on a mountain, not too far from here. Their power levels are faint, but you should be able to find them."

"Okay!" Wyler said, then disappeared into thin air with Scoop.

"You all handle these Drones. The two Queens are mine!" Menzuo said confidently.

"You got it!" Allucio answered.

"We got your back, dawg!" Desmurose jumped in.

"I'm going to make them pay for hurting my father!" Amiata snarled as they all floated to the ground.

As they did, all of the Drones followed them down.

"Make them suffer for everything that they have done to Earth! Have no Mercy on their dark souls. They deserve the pain," Master Renzfly yelled as they landed on the ground.

The red Queen smiled. "Do you really think that you can handle both of us by yourself?"

"There is no doubt in my mind," Menzuo responded confidently.

The smiles quickly left their faces. "Then we must finish our battle now!" the blue Queen shouted as they circled Menzuo, moving counter-clockwise.

"Let's go!" Menzuo yelled.

"We can do this, my Prince. Stay focused!" Solar shouted.

Menzuo nodded and kept his concentration on both Queens as they continued to circle him. He shook his head as he became agitated. "Get on with it, will you! Or are you two scared of what is about to happen?"

They both suddenly stopped. The blue Queen floated directly behind him as the red Queen floated right in front of his face. "I'm amazed by the confidence that you have gained. If you were my child, I would be a proud mother," the red Queen said.

"And I'd be sick to my stomach to see you as my mother. Shut up and just fight. I'm tired of listening to you two blab away!" Menzuo yelled.

Both of their horns started to glow with rage. "How dare you disrespect us?" the blue Queen yelled from behind.

"Get ready for your demise, Prince Menzuo!" the red Queen shouted.

Both Queens charged towards him, ready to take him out.

Just as they charged, a swarm of Drones flew towards the Solar Warriors that were just below. The epic battle for Earth's safety had begun, and the Huro bomb was on its way. Master Renzfly led the Solar Warriors against the Drones as Menzuo was ready to take on the Queens.

Chapter 13

The End of the Queens'

Each punch and kick that the blue Queen threw at Menzuo echoed loudly as he blocked them with ease. The next two punches missed.

"Is that all you've got? What a waste!" Menzuo mocked, making her angrier.

"Who do think you are?" the blue Queen screamed as Menzuo floated in front of her. He smiled, not responding to what she said. She backed up for a second. "You can't last that much longer!"

"You're right," Menzuo stated. "I don't have the time to waste. I have bigger problems than you to deal with."

The red Queen's eyes widened. "How dare you!" she shouted. "Time to see if you can handle the both of us!"

At that moment, both Queens charged from the front and back.

The Queens attacked the young Prince but to no avail. They couldn't break through his defense.

Menzuo quickly dropped one hand as he continued to block their attacks with the other. "I've had it with you two!" he screamed. The young warrior punched the blue Queen in the face and kicked the red Queen in the stomach. "It's my turn to finish this!"

As Menzuo took control of the battle with the Queens, the rest of the Solar Warriors continued to fight off the Drones. They all stood in a circle as millions of Pirates flew in from every direction. "Keep them back!" Master Renzfly shouted. "We could be at this for a long time, so hold your ground!"

"How's Menzuo doing?" Allucio yelled as he blasted a few hundred Drones away from him.

"We can't worry about that right now! He'll be fine!" Master Renzfly said as he continued with his attack. "Let's just hold up our part of this war!"

"Sonic Disk!"

"Fury Strike!"

Hundreds of Drones were blown away in an instant.

Princess Amiata looked up into the sky and noticed Menzuo taking control. "Hurry Menzuo, time is running out!" she shouted.

Within seconds, the entire city was flooded with Drones. The Solar Warriors were holding them off valiantly as Menzuo continued his attack with the Queens.

The young Prince continued to punch and kick both of the Queens. His energy level rose as they could not block any of his attacks. "Take This! Mega body attack!"

Three massive fireballs flew from his hands and blasted the blue Queen to the ground, near the edge of the city.

Menzuo kicked the red Queen in the stomach, making her hunch over and gasp for air. He looked at her as he studied her energy level. He could feel it getting weaker.

The blue Queen quickly regained her balance and charged from the ground. "You don't stand a chance!" she shouted as she got closer.

As the red Queen rose, she looked into Menzuo's eyes, very curious as to how he became so strong and confident. Before she could make another move, he punched her in the head as hard as he could.

Menzuo's strike was so violent that it knocked off her left horn, and smashed in her face.

"Aah, my face! My beautiful face!" she screamed as she covered it with her bruised hands.

As she flew closer, the blue Queen noticed what the young Prince had done to her sister. Her eyes widened with anger. "Take this!"

She swung right at Menzuo's head.

"Sensing Densor!" Menzuo shouted without even turning to see where the blue Queen was. He disappeared just as her fist was inches from his head.

"Where did he go?" the blue Queen said to herself. She looked over to her sister as she was still struggling with the pain that was delivered to her face.

"Aah, aah! My face!" the Red Queen continued to scream. "He's going to pay for that!" She lowered her hands as the Queen's face had sunk in. It looked as flat as a pancake.

"My lovely sister, what did he do to you?" the blue Queen said. Fear built in her voice. "Your face has been…"

"I know, and he will never survive this war because of this. I will have no mercy."

Both of the Queens floated with anger as they looked for Menzuo. As they paused in the sky, they both heard Master Renzfly shout out. "Mega body attack!"

This grabbed their attention, making them both look down.

"Noo!" the Queen's shouted.

Master Renzfly's blast killed off the last swarm of Pirate Drones. The ground was covered in black ooze from their fading bodies.

The Solar Warriors looked into the sky, noticing that Menzuo wasn't there. "Where is he?" Desmurose asked.

Master Renzfly smiled, knowing what was about to happen. "Just watch. The Queens are in for an extraordinary gift."

At that moment, Menzuo reappeared and caught the Queens off guard.

The young warrior Prince punched the red Queen in the face again just as violent as the last time. The blue Queen looked on in shock as the punch landed violently. As it did, the pearl separated from her forehead.

"Oh no, my pearl! My precious pearl!" the red Queen screamed loudly. Her body started to shake violently.

Menzuo and the blue Queen backed away. "Why did you do that? Why?" she continued to scream in pain as she held on to her face.

"What's happening?" Nuncio asked, seeing sparks fly from her body.

"Menzuo has found her weakness!" Master Renzfly said happily as his eyes widened. "Go for the pearl, Menzuo! That's the key!"

As the red Queen continued to scream, several sparks shot from her body. After a few seconds, the sky was filled with pink light.

"Eeyaah!"

Her body exploded. The loud blast shook the entire city.

The sky slowly went back to normal. A cloud of gray mist and a red dress were left to fall to the ground.

Menzuo looked to the blue Queen as she continued to back away with her hand up. "Now, now, my lovely Prince. Your point has been made. I will leave Earth and return all of the people," she said with a trembling voice. "You have proven yourself worthy."

Menzuo's shook his head without breaking a smile. "You leaving this planet, not good enough," he said as he slowly floated closer to her. "I will have no mercy on your stinking soul. You had no mercy for us. You tried your best to kill my friends and me, but you failed. You tried to kill Ambassador Naos and King Eojtaf, and you failed. You even tried to kill our parents, and failed again," Menzuo said as he floated closer. "Don't you get it? You're nothing but a failure, and your planet will always produce failures."

The Queen stopped trembling and yelled angrily as her one remaining horn brightened. "I am no failure! Passion Rush!"

"Never!" Menzuo shouted as the Queen released another attack.

As the pink and purple energy bomb flew towards him, Menzuo quickly powered up and absorbed it. Queen Eaziah was frozen as Menzuo sped towards her. He moved so swiftly that she couldn't react to his movement.

Her eyes widened with fear. "But how, how could you stop my attack?" she said with a shaky voice.

"Because I am the universal protector. Take this! Mega body attack!" he threw his massive bombs directly towards her, making all three explode right in her face.

As the smoke cleared, her skull was smashed in, just like her sisters. Queen Eaziah floated back in severe pain. "Why did you do this? I said that I would leave. I gave up. You defeated my sister. You won this battle," she said as she covered her face.

Menzuo quickly flew in and pushed the Queens' hands away from her eyes. "No, I have won the war!" without hesitation, he grabbed hold of the pearl that rested in the middle of her forehead.

No, no, do not pull it off! Please, noo!" she continued to plead with the young warrior as she scratched at his arm. Her horn quivered, showing her complete fear. The rest of her body dangled helplessly in the sky as it started to turn to stone. "Aah, aah! Please don't do this…aah!"

With no regard for her plea, Menzuo generated his energy into the palm of his right hand. "Good riddance, you evil beast!" he shouted as his hand vibrated from the enormous power that flowed within it. "Super mega body attack!" one huge flame flew from his palm and directly into Queen Eaziah's body.

"Noo! Eeyaah!" she screamed as her body disappeared.

The bright light from the blast blinded the Solar Warriors as they watched from below. "How did he do that?" Master Renzfly said as he tried his best to look through the bright light. "I never taught him that move. Unbelievable."

As the blinding attack faded, all that was left was a stone statue of Queen Eaziah's head. It floated in the sky right in front of the warrior Prince.

Menzuo opened his hand and looked at the pearl. "It is over," Menzuo said softly. He looked up and noticed the Queen's stone face in front of him. "Your reign of terror has ended," he let go of the pearl and watched it fall to the ground.

As the pearl fell, Queen Eaziah's solid face disintegrated with a calm breeze that blew past.

"He did it! He defeated the Queens!" Wyler shouted with joy.

"Yeah, Menzuo, you did it!" the rest of the Solar Warriors cheered as the young Prince floated to the ground.

Everyone looked up and noticed the pink fog that once covered the planet was now fading. "He really did it," Nuncio said with relief. "Menzuo has done it."

"No, we did it," Menzuo said as he landed next to his friends.

Everyone quickly surrounded him, all but Master Renzfly.

"I can't believe it! You destroyed the Queens all by yourself," Desmurose said immediately.

"That was too cool, man," Allucio jumped in. "I never doubted you, bro."

Princess Amiata and Nuncio bowed. "I am deeply honored to have fought by your side, Prince Menzuo," Amiata said as she raised her head.

"Yes, you are a true warrior," Nuncio added.

"Great job, Menzuo, I know it wasn't easy, but you did it," Scoop said as well.

After everyone congratulated him, Menzuo made his way over to Master Renzfly. "Thank you for coming with us," he said kindly.

Master Renzfly put his hand on Menzuo's shoulder. A smirk fell upon his face. "I couldn't let my pupil have all the fun saving his home planet, could I? Plus, I needed the exercise. It has been a very long time since I had a serious battle."

A smile fell upon Menzuo's face as well.

Naos and King Eojtaf finally made their way from the mountains and landed next to everyone. "Daddy!" Princess Amiata yelled happily as she ran over to him.

"Honey!" King Eojtaf said with a huge smile on his face. "Are you okay?"

Amiata jumped into her father's arms, hugging him as tight as she could. She placed her head onto his big shoulder. "Yes, I'm fine, father." Tears filled in her eyes. She slowly lifted her head. "We saw what you and Ambassador Naos did to stall the Queens. You guys did a great job."

Eojtaf chuckled as he looked at Naos. "Well, it didn't feel like a good job. Those Queens almost broke every bone in our bodies. If it wasn't for Wyler and Scoop, both of us would be on Legerdamien right now."

Ambassador Naos walked over to Menzuo, humbly and bowed respectfully. "You all have rid Earth of the Drones, and of the evil Pirate Queens. This is truly an unbelievable day. I thank you for giving your all to this planet," he looked up at the rest of the Solar Warriors. "You all will never be forgotten as the true protectors of this universe. My life is indebted to you."

Everyone bowed to Naos with complete respect for his courage to stand up in a battle that he knew he couldn't win.

"No, we honor you and King Eojtaf today," Master Renzfly said. "It is because of you two that we had a second chance. Both of you have the courage that cannot be matched, and we are proud to be in your presence."

Just as he said that a vast shadow covered the entire planet. "Everyone, look up," King Eojtaf shouted.

"Oh no, it's the Huro bomb!" Allucio shouted with his eyes wide.

Menzuo took a deep breath in complete frustration. "I forgot about that. What are we going to do?"

"After all of that hard work, Earth is still going to be destroyed," Desmurose growled.

"It doesn't look like we have enough time to leave this planet either," Wyler jumped in.

Menzuo dropped his head. "How could this be the end of Earth?" he said to himself. "I have to do something to stop it. I just have to."

Naos placed his hand on Menzuo's shoulder as he could sense his frustration. "I am sorry, Prince Menzuo. I know that you all have done your best, but there is nothing in this universe that can stop the Huro Bomb. Earth has no future," Naos said sadly.

As the bomb closed in on the planet, the Solar Warriors, along with Naos and Eojtaf, stood in silence, angrily waiting for the impact.

Menzuo started to breathe slowly as he lifted his head. "I have to try!" he shouted, grabbing everyone's attention. "I have to try!" he shot high into the sky.

Menzuo, wait!" Allucio yelled.

"No! Let him do this!" Master Renzfly responded as he stopped Allucio. "I believe that he has found a deep energy within him that may save us all."

"I hope so," Desmurose added as he looked on impatiently.

Higher and higher Menzuo flew into the sky. The Huro Bomb was now a few miles from Earth's atmosphere as Menzuo paused. The ground below rumbled forcefully as he looked directly into the bomb. "What am I going to do, Solar?"

"We have to figure something out, my Prince," Solar responded. "Whatever we do, we better figure it out quickly because that bomb is almost here!"

The flames from the Huro Bomb were flickering violently as it got closer. The heat that the bomb was giving off was getting stronger.

At that moment, the blue diamond started to vibrate. Sparks shot out of it in every direction. "Ouch! What's happening, Solar? What's happening? Aah!" Menzuo screamed out in pain.

"I...I don't...don't know! I can't control this energy surge! Everything is expanding around me! It's getting too big!" Solar shouted.

The Solar Warriors watched Menzuo as his body was encased with a blue force field. "What's happening to him?" Amiata yelled.

Master Renzfly shook his head. "I don't know, be patient. We have to wait and see."

A loud, humming sound filled the sky. It was coming from the Huro bomb, and it was getting louder as it got closer. Menzuo looked down and noticed the blue diamond spinning within the clasp. "Aah! Solar! What's it doing?" Menzuo shouted.

"I don't know, but something is building up in here, and it is huge!" Solar yelled. "I have no control over this, my Prince!"

A white light shot out of the diamond. The force field that encased them quickly faded. Menzuo's power suit started to pulsate with a bright white light, growing all around him.

"Solar!" Menzuo shouted.

The white light completely brightened the sky and covered Menzuo.

"It can't be!" Master Renzfly shouted. "It can't be."

"What is that?" Allucio shouted as he covered his eyes from the bright light.

"No warrior has ever achieved such great levels of power. Menzuo has somehow unlocked the spirits of the past warrior's. This is unbelievable."

Everyone tried to look up as they squinted their eyes. Trying to see what was taking place in the sky.

"Something is happening, Menzuo," Solar shouted.

Menzuo's power suit was now completely white. An immense energy shot through him and Solar, calming their fears. The rumbling from the Huro bomb silenced.

Menzuo looked at his hands and the rest of his body, noticing a golden glow coming from the creases of his suit. A golden mist covered his body as he looked at the Huro bomb, closing in.

"Release it, Prince Menzuo," the voice of Master Kane spoke to him.

The young Prince held out his hands and closed his eyes. "Here we go, Solar!" Menzuo shouted.

"Do it!" Solar yelled.

"Haa!" a golden beam shot out from Menzuo's body, directly into the center of the Huro bomb as it was just a few seconds from entering the planet's atmosphere.

The golden beam quickly incased the Huro Bomb, making it stop just above the planet. As the golden light took complete control over the Huro bomb, everyone below noticed that it started to shrink. "He stopped it," Princess Amiata shouted. "Menzuo stopped the Huro bomb."

As the bomb shrunk to the size of a pea, Menzuo's body started to relax. The blue diamond slowly went back to its normal state, and his white power suit faded. Menzuo was back to normal as well. "What...what just happened, Solar?" Menzuo said curiously as he shook his head.

"I have no idea," Solar responded. "I don't know what that energy was, but I believe Master Kane has something to do with it."

"Um, Master Renzfly?" Allucio questioned. "Is this a good thing or a bad thing?"

"I don't know, but this feels very eerie," Master Renzfly said as he kept his eyes on Menzuo.

The young warrior continued to float above his friends, as he tried to figure out what was going on. "I think we did it, Solar!"

"I think we did, my Prince!" Solar responded with relief.

A few seconds later, a loud explosion shook the planet. The sky brightened with an abundance of fireworks.

"Whoa!" Naos shouted as he stumbled back. The sky was filled with many different colors. "My goodness, Prince Menzuo did it, he saved the planet!" Naos' eyes were as wide as they could get. "This is truly unbelievable!" he said as he looked into the sky.

Master Renzfly watched Menzuo float in place as the fireworks exploded above their heads. "That young warrior has surpassed everything that I could have ever taught him in such a short amount of time. He truly is ready to be the universal protector."

Menzuo smiled as he watched the beautiful show that was just above him.

"Menzuo," Solar screamed out. "Something else is building up in here!"

The smile quickly left Menzuo's face as he looked down at the diamond. "What is it, Solar?"

In an instant, three huge blue waves flew out of the diamond and filled the sky.

"What in the world is that?" Amiata shouted curiously as she looked on with the others.

Everyone stood in silence. They watched four more blue waves fly from Menzuo's body. The waves flew clear across the northeast of the country. As the sky was completely covered with a mist, everyone watched as it fell towards the ground like snow.

Shiny crystal's sparkled from within the blue haze. "What is this?" Scoop asked.

Before anyone could answer, they all heard Menzuo scream. "Solar!"

With Menzuo's cry, the waves stopped falling. Everyone below looked up and noticed their friend's body go limp. As it did, he started to drop out of the sky in the distance.

"Noo, Menzuo!" Desmurose shouted. He took off into the air as he watched his friend continue to fall.

"Come on, everyone, let's go!" Allucio yelled out as he shot up into the sky.

The rest of the warriors followed closely behind.

Menzuo's body slammed into a field in one area of the city.

"I hope he is okay," Amiata said quickly.

"I do hope so, my Princess," Nuncio answered.

Within a few seconds, the warriors landed next to Menzuo as he was planted into the ground. He was unconscious and completely motionless. Princess Amiata knelt down next to him and stroked his face. "Prince Menzuo, please wake up. You did it, you saved planet Earth. It is all over. You did it."

Right after she spoke, the blue diamond started to shake. Allucio looked on, curious to see what was going to happen. "What is it doing?"

Princess Amiata stood and backed away. "I don't know, I hope that it doesn't explode."

The diamond started to shine. It was too bright for anyone of them to look at. They all covered their eyes. Very shortly, the light-filled the area.

The wind blew passed their faces then instantly stopped. As it did, the light faded, and the blue diamond went motionless.

"I wonder what that was," Allucio asked.

"Look, something is happening to it," Wyler pointed out.

Everyone noticed the diamond melting into Menzuo's suit. "It is gone. Just like that, it's gone," Nuncio said. He was in shock as a blue glow filled Menzuo's body.

The entire city was still filled with the blue waves, but everyone kept their eyes on the young Prince.

Within seconds, Menzuo popped up and inhaled as much air as he could. His eyes were wide as he started to breathe rapidly.

Master Renzfly put his hand on Menzuo's shoulder. "My Prince, calm yourself, are you okay?"

Menzuo nodded as he reached for the blue diamond. He ran his fingers across his neck, searching for it. He quickly looked down and noticed that it was gone. "Where is it? Where is the diamond? It's not here? It must have fallen off!" he shouted as he quickly jumped to his feet. "I have to find it."

Scoop shook his head. "Prince Menzuo, it melted into your suit. That was the last time we saw it."

Menzuo quickly looked around as his heart pounded rapidly. "Then where's Solar? Is he gone, too?"

Ambassador Naos stepped forward. "We didn't see him when you fell. I am sorry, I believe that he is gone, my Prince."

Allucio and Desmurose walked over their friend and put their hands on his shoulders. "I'm sorry, Menzuo. I know how much he meant to you," Allucio said sadly.

"Hey, just look at it this way, now he's a part of you, that's better than having him completely gone, right?"

Menzuo dropped his head and nodded. A tear rolled off of his cheek as Master Renzfly spoke strongly. "Prince Menzuo, hold your head up high. Solar left us for a good cause, but he will always be with you, now, more than ever.

"But Master Kane said that I had to promise to go back to Legerdamien with Solar. How can I do that now?"

Master Renzfly put his hand on Menzuo's chest. "You will keep Solar in your heart as you return. That is how you will go back."

Menzuo shook his head. "But I don't understand how this has happened. It doesn't make any sense."

"Maybe it was supposed to be this way," Master Renzfly added. "Maybe that was part of the gift that Master Kane gave you. Maybe, this is his way of starting your training. Be very proud that you and Solar have saved this planet, and move forward. You owe him that much."

"Yes," King Eojtaf jumped in. "You should be extremely proud of what you and Solar have accomplished in such a short time. You never gave up in any of your battles with the Pirate Warriors. Not even when everything was against you. Both of you kept your spirits up, and you faced your fears. Not many people can do that."

A strained smile went across Menzuo's face as he looked at the city in the distance. It continued to burn from the destruction. He sighed heavily. "Look at this. All of the people who once lived on this planet are still gone. Everything is ruined," he turned to everyone, now furious as he thought of what the people were going through. "What did I save? Nothing will be the same, nothing."

Ambassador Naos sighed. "It is never a loss, my Prince. We just have to have a little faith in getting our people back, and rebuilding this planet. It is one cycle in life that we can fix."

As Naos finished speaking, Menzuo thought about the people that were lost in this war, including Jessica. She had to suffer through this carnage and was now in a life of slavery on a mutant planet. One massive tear fell from his cheek and hit the grass in front of him. As it did, the liquid mixed with the blue waves that were settled on the ground. A stiff breeze quickly picked up and blew past all of them.

"What is this?" Desmurose asked.

As the wind continued to circulate through the city, everyone heard Master Kane's deep voice call out from the sky. "After a time of pain and struggle, peace will find its way through and bring life home, where it belongs."

Everyone continued to look into the sky, very confused as the clouds moved in circles. King Scoop was the only one still looking at the ground. He noticed something extraordinary beginning to take place. "Look, everyone, the planet is beginning to heal itself."

The great warriors glanced down, then quickly looked in the distance and noticed that all of the burning buildings and the destroyed city going back to its original state.

Menzuo's mouth dropped. "This is the real final gift of the blue diamond," he said happily.

The ground shook as the blue waves rose up to their waists. The waves moved with the gentle wind. Everything at that moment started to rebuild itself. Every crushed car and demolished street slowly went back to normal. It was as if someone had pressed a rewind button.

"I can't believe what I am seeing!" Ambassador Naos said.

Menzuo smiled happily as he could feel the city around him going back to what it was before he had left to planet Bralose.

The pain that Ambassador Naos was feeling for planet Earth was beginning to fade. He could feel its energy coming back. "This is my beautiful world," he said with a smile as he looked at Menzuo, Allucio, and Desmurose. "Our beautiful world!" he took a deep breath of fresh air and let it out slowly.

A few moments later, the wind stopped, and the blue waves faded. Before they could say another word, the entire northeast of the country was back to its original state. "Thank you, Master Kane," Menzuo said. A calm joy flowed through him.

Desmurose shouted. "This is great!" he paused as he thought a little more, "But what about all of the people? They're still gone."

As soon as spoke, one by one, each and every person who was kidnapped started to reappear back to where they last were. They were all terrified, and some were still screaming. The sights that they had witnessed on planet Excervo were still fresh in their minds.

"They're back! But how, how did this happen?" Menzuo asked curiously.

Ambassador Naos pointed to Menzuo's feet. "It was because of you," he said as Menzuo looked down. He noticed that the ground was glowing around his feet. He looked back up as Naos continued. "That single tear of pain and sorrow that fell from your eye has given life on Earth another chance. I guess that, with the combined energy of the blue diamond, and how much you care about this planet, made it happen."

Menzuo looked up with a smile. "This is unbelievable. Everything is going to be okay!"

"You've got that right!" a familiar voice spoke out from above.

Everyone quickly looked up and noticed a figure floating down towards them. He was wearing a power suit, similar to Menzuo and the other warriors.

"Solar?" Menzuo shouted as his brother landed.

"Yeah, who did you think it was, Santa Clause?" Solar responded jokingly.

"I can't believe this. I thought that you were gone forever," Menzuo answered.

"Yeah, me too," Solar responded. "I was shot out of the blue diamond with the blue waves. Once I was out, something strange started to happen. I heard a voice speak to me. It said, for my courageous heart, I would become completely whole again. I was able to gain control of the waves and was able to send them towards the ground, and to tell you something, it felt excellent to control that energy."

Menzuo hugged Solar as tight as he could. "This is great! So this means that you are alive and do not have to live in the blue diamond anymore."

"I...I guess so," Solar said with a smile. His face slowly dropped as he realized he and Menzuo wouldn't be fighting together any longer. "I guess that blue diamond was meant to do a lot of great things, and to separate us as well."

Menzuo let go of Solar and nodded. "I'm just happy that you're not gone forever. I don't know what I would have done."

They all stood in the field as the people of Earth were slowly returning. The blue waves quickly swiped the ground and lifted high into the sky. It took all of the bad memories of the past events out of the minds of the people.

Menzuo jumped as he remembered something. "Oh, man, our parents! They're still on the moon!"

Allucio's eyes widened. "Oh yeah, they were stuck on the moon this whole time."

"I think it is okay to bring them back," Desmurose added.

Nuncio rubbed his fingers together, making a small control appear. He pressed the button and smiled. "They will be back at your house, Menzuo, by the time we get there."

"Well, everyone," Ambassador Naos said quickly, "I think we'd better disappear and get over there before someone notices us. We don't want to scare people more than they have been already."

People with picnic baskets were walking up the hill towards them.

Just before the group reached the top of the hill, Master Renzfly shouted. "Mega Sensing Densor!" the Solar Warriors disappeared and headed to Menzuo's parent's backyard.

Chapter 14

Breaking the News

Menzuo and the team reappeared in his backyard. They looked around cautiously, hoping that no one would see them. "I think we're safe," Allucio said.

"Okay, guys, we're about to go into the kitchen. Our parents are sitting at the table talking," Menzuo said.

"It looks like our parents are trying to explain everything to yours, Menzuo," Allucio responded.

Menzuo made his power suit disappear. Allucio and Desmurose did the same.

"You all stay out here," Michael said to Master Renzfly and the others.

Jammal, Michael, and Jeffery walked to the door. "We'll call you guys in, in a minute," Jeffery stated.

Everyone nodded as they opened the door and walked into the house.

"Please tell me again, what just happened," Steven said, still very confused. "The last thing that I remember was being on the freaking moon, and now we're back in the kitchen that I thought blew up. Either I'm going crazy, or something peculiar is going on."

"I can explain that dad," Jammal responded. He walked into the kitchen with Jeffery and Michael close behind.

Krystal jumped up out of her chair, "Honey, are you're okay?" she ran over to him with Barkley by her side.

"Hey, kid," Barkley said as he licked Jammal's hand. "I see you did great against those Queens."

Jammal nodded, then stroked his dogs head. He didn't want to say anything and scare his parents.

Jeffrey and Michael's mothers' ran over to them as well. "Oh, thank goodness you're okay," Stacy spoke.

"I was so worried about you," Marianne added. A tear fell from her face.

"We're okay, mom," Jammal responded. Krystal continued to hold onto him very tight. Jammal slowly pulled away. "I think you guys better take a seat. We have a lot of explaining to do."

All of the parents sat down slowly. "What is it, honey?" Krystal asked. "Is it about what your father and I think has happened on this planet?"

Jammal nodded as he looked at Jeffery and Michael. "You guys don't remember anything?"

"Their minds were somewhat erased just a few minutes ago," Michael Sr. answered. "They only know bits and pieces of what happened. You'll be explaining this to them as if it were their first time hearing it."

Jammal nodded. "Well, yes it is, mom," he turned to Jeffery and Michael. "I guess there is no easy way to explain it then, huh?"

"Nope, we should just let the others in," Jeffery added.

"Let who in? What others?" Steven asked curiously.

Michael opened the door. All of the warriors walked into the kitchen, trying not to scare Jammal's parents. "Son, who...who are these...people?" Steven shouted. He sat back in his chair.

Jammal looked at Jeffery and Michael again then back to his parent. "I guess we should show them," Jammal said.

In a blink of an eye, Jeffery and Michael made their power suits return with Jammal doing the same.

Steven and Krystal's eyes widened as they watched their clothes change. "So, this is for real?" Steven answered.

Krystal grabbed hold of her husband's hand and looked at all of the different warriors who were standing in her kitchen.

Jammal walked over to his parents as his power suit faded. Jeffery and Michael did the same. "Mom, dad, my real name isn't Jammal. I am known as the protector of the universe. These are all of my friends who fight with me," he pointed from left to right. "This is Princess Amiata, her father, King Eojtaf. This is Nuncio, the Princess's guardian. This is the form King of planet Walonoke, Scoop, and he fights with Wyler the Whistler. This is Ambassador Naos of Earth, and this is Solar. Jeffery and Michael are also a part of this team. We are called the Solar Warriors."

It was quiet for a few seconds as Krystal looked for the right words to say. "Is this some type of joke?"

"This is far from any joke," Marianne replied, trying to calm her friend down. "What Menzuo is telling you, is very true."

Krystal looked at her, shocked. "And how do you know that?"

George O'Conner leaned forward. "That is because we are all a part of Menzuo's destiny."

"Menzuo? I think that you said that name on the spaceship when we were on the moon, but who's Menzuo?" Steven asked. He tried his best to remember if everything that took place was real.

"That's my real name, dad. That was my given birth name," Jammal answered.

Steven looked over at him. "How long have you known this?"

"About a week before my twelfth birthday," Jammal responded. He sat in a chair next to his parents. "What happened to you on the moon was real. We were able to save you from the war that was happening on Earth."

"So that floating lady was real, and the pink fog that covered the planet was real?" Steven asked.

"Yes, it was, dad, but it is okay now," Jammal responded.

Krystal covered her eyes. "This must be a dream. How can all of this be real?"

Jammal lowered her hands from her face. "Mom, everything is real. It is all real. These people, the evil Queen, the pink cloud covering the planet, all of it."

Steven sighed heavily. He continued to sit in shock, looking at the Solar Warriors as they stood patiently, without making any startling movements. "Let me guess, you all are not from this planet, right?"

"All but Ambassador Naos," Michael answered.

Steven looked over to Naos and turned his face up. "Man, you look really familiar?" he studied his face for a few more seconds. "You look like that rapper, Busted something?"

Naos smiled. "It's Busta, and that is me. That is my disguise on this planet. It's the best way for me to blend in with the people and keep my true identity hidden."

Steven shook his head. He directed his attention back to Jammal. "Okay, son, please explain all of this to your mother and me. First off, how did we end up on the moon? Second, what was that thing that was in the sky? All that I remember is seeing a pink cloud flying towards us and me passing out in a tunnel that was hidden in our basement. Then seeing the pink cloud from the moon. It's all fuzzy."

Jammal started to pet Barkley as Krystal spoke. "Barkley saved all of us from that thing. He knew something was wrong, right when he saw it. Is he in on this as well?"

"I'll explain everything. Let's move into the living room, where it's a little more comfortable. There is more space in there for all of us to sit."

Everyone walked into the living room. The Solar Warriors looked around in awe as they studied the house. "This is very small compared to our castle," Amiata whispered to her father.

"Well, most humans live like this. It is the norm on planet Earth. Not everyone is royalty," Eojtaf said to his daughter in a soft tone.

"But it is so cozy. It feels like a great place to live," Nuncio added.

Jeffery and Michael chuckled as they listened to their conversation. "I guess this is the first time they have been in an Earth house," Michael replied.

"I know. It's something for them to get used to," Jeffery answered.

As everyone found a seat, Jammal started his explanation of past events. "Well, dad, it all started the week before my twelfth birthday. That was when I found out that I was adopted, you remember. I was told about where I came from and the path that was ahead of me. The person who told me all of this was my older brother," Jammal said. Solar walked forward as he continued. "This is my brother, Solar."

Steven shook his hand. "Nice to meet you?"

Solar bowed. "It is my honor to finally meet both of you as well. You all have done a great job raising Prince Menzuo."

Steven sat back with a perplexed look on his face. "Prince?" he said, then looked at Jammal. "I do remember someone telling your mom and me that you were a Prince, is that true?"

"Yes, I am. Let me explain it to you. When I was a baby, my father, the King of planet Yardania, had no choice but to send me to the safest planet in the universe, far away from planet Excervo. Earth was the only planet that was safe enough to keep me out of harm's way. He also sent me here to protect the planet from any evil. When I found out about my powers, I guess protecting the Earth was more than what I was going to be given."

"I remember seeing something about that in a spaceship. I guess it wasn't a dream. So, you've been battling aliens or something?" Krystal asked.

"Not aliens, Pirate Warriors, from the planet Excervo." Jeffery jumped in.

"Yardania? Excervo? King Zenshuo? All of this seems so unreal," Steven answered.

"The universe is much larger than you could ever imagine Mr. and Mrs. Hall," Michael added.

"So, what Pirate Warriors have you been battling?" Krystal asked.

"The first one that I had to fight was known as Morbid. On my twelfth birthday, he was trying to take over Earth and the power of all good and evil. After Solar and I beat him, Earth was safe for a while. Just recently, we returned from Planet Bralose. Solar and I had to go to that planet to fight Hydrosion, a new Pirate Warrior that was released. Princess Amiata sent Nuncio, her guardian, and protector to Earth and asked for my help. During my battle against Hydrosion, we found out that Earth was taken over by Queen Eaziah. You know, that lady you saw floating in the sky? Unfortunately, we fell into trouble with the Queen. Ambassador Naos and King Eojtaf had to jump in and help," Jammal paused with a smile. He looked at his friends full of confidence.

He then looked back at his parents. They were utterly glued in. "Keep going, this is really weird, but we want to hear more," Steven said.

Jammal continued. "After we beat Hydrosion, we found out about the Pirate Queen's plan to take over Earth. That was when we came back here to fight for the safety of the planet. So that's it in a nutshell...the quick version."

Everyone sat in the room, waiting for Jammal's parents to respond. They both had looks of confusion as Jammal stopped speaking. It was as if they were trying their best to let it sink in.

Steven looked at everyone as they smiled back. "You know, I do believe that all of this is true. How did we end up on the moon again?"

"Oh," Michael jumped in. "When we came back to Earth, we found you guys under the house."

"Our house really did blow up?" Krystal asked.

"Yes and everything was destroyed, the houses, the buildings, and the entire city. We got you all out and put you on the ship. That's how you ended up on the moon."

Steven shook his head. "This is crazy," he said. He continued to look at everyone in his living room. "So, our universe is bigger than we think?"

"Oh yeah, Mr. Hall," Jeffery replied.

"How did you prepare for all of this?" Krystal asked. "You have school, and you're always with your friends or at home. What did you do?"

"I trained in my sleep with Solar. Up until now, Solar fought with me from inside of the diamond that was around my neck. Now, he has his life back. Master Renzfly is my trainer. He is the one who taught me the Yardanian fighting style." Jammal looked at him with a satisfied smile.

Steven sighed very hard and stood. "I think I need some coffee," he walked passed everyone and into the kitchen.

Jammal and the others continued to explain everything to his parents for hours on end. Everything seemed as if it was still a dream to Steven and Krystal.

They sat back on the couch in awe and drank their coffee as they continued to listen to the stories. From King Zenshuo deciding the fate of the universe, to the existing planets in the outer realm. Steven and Krystal knew that it was going to take some time to understand, but they were willing to listen.

Jammal's parents were beginning to feel a little at ease. Still, the news of their son being the universal protector completely confused them. Jammal was happy to be able to tell his parents who he was and what his life's mission entailed.

Chapter 15

Lord Fetid's Warning

"This is unbelievable," Steven said as he fell back onto the couch. "What is the next move for all of you?"

As Steven spoke, a tremendous rumble shook the Earth. The bright sky was quickly filled with rolling black clouds. The ease of happiness promptly left the living room.

"What's going on?" Krystal asked. She turned around and looked out of the window.

A dark shadow passed over the house. A sharp pain quickly hit Jammal's stomach. He and the others rapidly stood.

"This doesn't feel good, Menzuo," Solar cautioned.

Barkley growled and moved in front of Krystal and Steven, ready to protect them again.

"Menzuo, show yourself!" a deep cold voice shouted loudly.

Jammal looked at his parents. "Mom, dad, stay in here," he turned to the others. "Come on, guys, let's see what this is about," they ran through the kitchen and out into the backyard.

Everyone around the city stopped and looked into the dark sky, they heard the voice call out again. "Menzuo, you have angered Lord Fetid!"

As Jammal stood in his yard with his friends, they quickly powered up and got ready for another battle.

A colossal face appeared from the dark clouds and focused in on the Solar Warriors. "It's Lord Fetid!" Master Renzfly yelled.

"What is he doing here?" Menzuo said curiously. "I thought he couldn't leave Excervo?"

"It looks like things are changing," Allucio shouted.

"Prince Menzuo, your weakness in battle has given planet Excervo an amazing amount of power. As I speak, my planet is growing stronger. Lord Fetid spoke loudly.

The people throughout the east coast of the country stood in confusion as Lord Fetid's face formed in the clouds. Green lights beamed down from his eyes, onto the people below. No one could believe what they were seeing. The television crews were filming the face in the clouds as the thunderous booms rang from the sky.

"What we are seeing is something out of the ordinary people," one of the news reporters shouted into the microphone. "This mysterious face just appeared in the sky, yelling out for someone named Menzuo? Who is this person, and what does he want? We will be here to cover this exclusive story to the very end."

As the wind picked up, the fury within Menzuo started to build. "That's it! If he wants to see me, he can see me face to face!" He shot up into the sky as fast as he could.

"Menzuo, No!" Master Renzfly screamed.

All of the people in Springfield noticed the young warrior flying up towards the dark face. "What is that?" one person shouted quickly.

The news cameras were set up and filming everything that was happening. "This is unreal!" one reporter shouted. "This will be the story of a lifetime! Please pay close attention, people. I don't believe this! Someone is actually flying towards the face in the clouds! We have a real superhero living right here in Springfield, Massachusetts. This is the first one to be found outside of Hero City."

Menzuo continued to fly towards Lord Fetid's face with anger building inside of him.

"Within seven Earth years," Lord Fetid spoke as Menzuo flew closer, "planet Excervo will become the strongest world within the universe. Then I, Lord Fetid, and my Pirate Drones will take over all planets. This useless Earth will be destroyed, and all others will bow down to my rule."

"I'll take care of you right now!" Menzuo shouted.

Lord Fetid's face focused in on Menzuo as he flew closer. His smile widened in the clouds. "Aah, there you are!" he said in a bone-chilling tone. "You just couldn't resist, could you?"

Without hesitation, Menzuo went into battle. "Mega body attack!" His bombs were quickly stopped by Lord Fetid. His body was frozen in place high in the sky. "I...I can't move!"

"Let me show you what will become of this universe under my reign," Lord Fetid yelled out.

A stream of black smoke quickly surrounded Menzuo. The smoke went into his nose and into his mouth. Lord Fetid had tapped into Menzuo's brain, connecting his vision of the future to Menzuo's thoughts.

"Aaah, what is this?" Menzuo screamed violently as he lost control over his mind. "Get out of my head! Get out now, Aaah!"

Views of carnage and all-out war filled the young Prince's thoughts. Lord Fetid's strategic plan to take over the universe was seen as clear as if Menzuo was standing right in the middle of it with no power to make it stop. The first vision was the eradication of Yardania. A Magna vortex was opened to the universe that led to uniting Excervo with an evil counterpart, an unknown and uncontrollable evil.

"Noo!" Menzuo screamed as he grabbed hold of his head.

An all mighty war broke out within the universe and was controlled by the hands of Lord Fetid. Pirate Drones fought side by side with an unknown evil. Visions of the Solar Warriors falling at his evil hands, made Menzuo's heart beat faster.

"Aah, noo!" Menzuo continued to scream frantically.

"I should take your soul now, you helpless fool!" Lord Fetid shouted as the visions of the near future continued to play in Menzuo's mind. A black hand formed from the stream of smoke.

"This can't happen. This is no future! No way!" Menzuo screamed as Lord Fetid's hand moved closer.

"But it will happen, Prince Menzuo! I can show you how powerful my evil can be!" Lord Fetid responded. He released a stream of green mist into Menzuo's eyes.

A loud explosion filled the sky, making the ground shake below. "Oh my goodness, it looks like the flying person up there is not going to make it," the reporter said. "I don't know if I should be afraid or if I should just keep watching. I don't know what to do!"

"Aaah!" Menzuo screamed at the top of his lungs as the green mist fully entered his eyes. His screams were heard by everyone below.

"This is not good!" Scoop said as he watched from below.

"Noo!" Menzuo shouted again as another picture flew through his mind.

Visions of his parents and friends being disintegrated flooded his thoughts. Sights of several planets blowing up one by one shot passed him. The loud explosions squeezed his brain. He could feel every bit of the pain that Lord Fetid was delivering throughout the universe.

"That's enough!" Master Renzfly shouted loudly. He rushed to Menzuo's aide as fast as he could. Solar followed closely behind.

Lord Fetid's cold hand grabbed hold of Menzuo's head. "Come, my Prince! Your body and power will belong to me for all eternity."

"Noo!" Menzuo screamed as he floated in severe pain.

"Oh my!" the reporter shouted. "There are more of these flying people going up to the face! I can't believe what I am seeing!"

"Dark knight attack!" Master Renzfly shouted.

A silver blade flew from his hand, directly at Lord Fetid's arm.

Menzuo was utterly paralyzed. His body dangled in the sky as all of Earth watched in fear.

"Solar flare!" Solar shouted.

He threw a giant fireball with Master Renzfly's attack.

"Your energy is unbelievable!" Lord Fetid shouted. "A child, this strong is not regular! I will enjoy regenerating myself as the new universal ruler! No one will ever defeat me!"

The silver blade that Master Renzfly threw cut right through Lord Fetid's smoked hand, disconnecting it from Menzuo's head.

Solar's attack pushed the mist back into the cloud.

"Noo!" Lord Fetid screamed. "I am too close to taking over this warrior, he is mine!"

Menzuo's limp body fell down towards the ground.

"Go away, you beast! You are not welcomed here!" Master Renzfly shouted. Allucio, Desmurose, and the others flew up next to him.

"You will never control this universe!" Desmurose shouted alongside Master Renzfly.

"Everyone, give him all that you've got!" Master Renzfly shouted.

Everyone's hands were glowing violently. They directed them right at Lord Fetid's face. "Let your attacks go!" Solar screamed.

The Solar Warrior's, along with King Eojtaf and Ambassador Naos threw their bombs directly at Lord Fetid's face. Each one of their energy attacks exploded on contact.

"Noo, noo! I am not strong enough to fight this battle!" Lord Fetid said. His face started to fade. "I will return when the time is right! This universe is mine!" his face completely disappeared into the dark clouds.

As it did, the clouds rolled away, letting the sunlight shine through once again.

Amiata looked down and noticed Menzuo lying in a field near his house. "I think we better get to him."

"Let's go!" Desmurose added.

They all quickly disappeared from the sky.

"Whoa! Did you get that?" the reporter said to his cameraman. "I'm going to be a megastar with this story!"

A crowd of people surrounded Menzuo as he was implanted and unconscious in the middle of the field. "Look, mommy," a little boy said. "It's the guy who was in the sky.

Everyone looked at Menzuo's face. "He looks like he's just a kid," an older man said out loud.

As everyone stood around the warrior, Jessica, Maiah, and Monique made their way through the crowd to get a better look at him.

"I wonder who it is," Monique said as they pushed through the crowd.

As soon as they made their way through, Jessica looked at Menzuo. It was something about the young warriors face. "Look, girls, he looks so familiar," Jessica whispered to the twins.

Maiah looked on with a scrunched face. "I know, but who could it be?"

As Jessica continued to study the warriors face, she noticed a small mark on his neck. "That must have happened when he hit the ground," she said to herself. She was trying hard to keep everything in her mind as the crowd continued to form around the fallen warrior.

As everyone continued to look on, the Solar Warriors appeared around Menzuo.

"Whoa! The crowd of people shouted as they jumped back.

Solar quickly picked Menzuo up as everyone looked on at the group of warriors. No one was afraid of them, but they were still cautious.

"Mega Sensing Densor!" Master Renzfly shouted.

In an instant, everyone disappeared. "Where did they go?" Jessica asked as she moved to the center of the circle.

"I have no clue, but that was really cool," Monique said with her eyes wide.

Jessica looked down and noticed a small piece of cloth that was on the ground where the warrior was lying. She picked it up and slowly placed it in her pocket, and looking into the sky as the crowd slowly dispersed. Everyone in the city was nervous and didn't know what to do.

A few moments later, the Solar Warriors reappeared back in Jammal's backyard. They all powered down. "Let's get into the house before someone sees us," Jeffery said.

Jeffery and Michael quickly changed back to their Earth clothes. They walked into the kitchen with the others as Solar held onto Menzuo.

Chapter 16

Heading Home

"Oh, my Goodness!" Steven said frantically, "What's happened to him?"

Solar put Menzuo on the couch. "Scoop, can you revive him?"

Scoop walked over. Krystal held tightly to Steven as she cried for her son's safety. "Oh, please be okay. He's not dead, is he?" she asked.

"I doubt it," Solar responded, "but he has been seriously injured. Hopefully, Scoop can fix this."

Scoop held his hands over Menzuo's body. An orange glow quickly filled his palms and fell onto Menzuo chest. As it faded, Scoop backed away. "He should be fine in a moment."

A few seconds later, Menzuo slowly woke. "Uh, what happened?" He grabbed hold of his head. As he did, a flash of Lord Fetid's future rushed his mind then quickly left. "Whoa!"

"Oh, thank goodness," Krystal said as she hugged her son, relieved to see him waking.

His power suit slowly faded. "Oh, man! That wasn't fun at all," Jammal said as he sat up. "If what Lord Fetid showed me comes true, then we all have some big problems in the future."

"Then we must prepare ourselves. Do you know how much time we have left before he returns?" Master Renzfly asked curiously.

"Lord Fetid said seven years from now, but some of the events that he showed me seemed like it was taking place before he made his final return. Something happens while Excervo is still generating its energy. I don't know what or when, but it really didn't look to favor us at all."

Steven quickly looked at the television. "Look, everyone. What just happened out there is already on the news!"

"Turn it up," Michael Sr. said.

The report was showing the face of Lord Fetid floating in the sky as the stream of black smoke grabbed hold of

Menzuo. "So that's what happened," Jammal said as he looked on.

The Solar Warriors were flying up close behind, shooting their attacks at Lord Fetid's face. As Fetid disappeared back into the clouds, the sun found its way out, shining on the people below.

The reporter spoke. "There you have it, ladies and gentlemen. Today is the day that all of Earth now knows that we are not alone in the universe. There are more heroes outside of Hero City. Who were those mysterious people flying in the sky? We all heard the scary voice ask for someone called Menzuo. Who is this person, and is he here to save Earth or to destroy it? Does this mean universal peace or the destruction of our planet? More on this story at eleven."

Steven turned the television off. "Oh man, everyone on this planet is going to go bonkers with this coming out, aren't they?"

Ambassador Naos nodded. "Yes, and with all that is already taking place in Hero City, this will only heighten the fear of true heroes within our world. Just the thought of living out in the universe is going to send this planet into a state of craziness. The fanatics will hit the streets, and Earth will become a very different place after today."

"What are we going to do?" Jammal asked. "People are going to want answers. They know my name, and I don't want them thinking that I am some type of bad person."

"Don't worry about that right now, Prince Menzuo. People know your real name, but not your identity. You are still a mystery to this world," Naos said confidently. "I will handle getting the message about you out to them. I will give the people of Earth only what is needed. It's the same thing that I had to do for Hero City. As long as people get decent information, all will be calm. I just have to contact the correct people."

"Ambassador Naos can handle this world, my Prince," Master Renzfly said. "He has been doing this for centuries. We have to worry about keeping your identity safe. Until we meet with Lord Fetid and planet Excervo, you, Allucio, and Desmurose must act like you are just as surprised by the new findings."

"We understand, Master Renzfly," Jeffery responded.

"Yeah, we understand," Michael followed.

"Oh, by the way," Jammal added. He looked over to Naos. "Speaking of Hero City, someone named Paladin called on me. I think he needs my help."

Naos' placed his hand onto his chin. "That is strange. Things in Hero City seem to be peaceful at the moment. Are you sure that Paladin called on you?"

"Yes, he visited me while I was sleep on planet Bralose. That's when I saw visions on Queen Eaziah as well."

"That is strange indeed," Ambassador Naos answered. "I will keep an eye on Hero City. You need to recover from this war. You've battled two massively strong Pirate Warrior's in a short amount of time. I don't think that it would be wise for you to travel to Hero City at the moment. Plus all eye are on Menzuo so, you need to lay low and keep your identity hidden."

"But what about Paladin's message?" Jammal asked.

"I will keep an eye on Hero City for you and will keep you updated if anything changes," Naos responded.

"Thank you Ambassador Naos. I think I do need a moment to rest and gather my thoughts. Everything that Lord Fetid has shown me really has me worried. Also, not having Solar fight with me is the biggest change that has happened."

Solar stepped forward. "It is okay, Menzuo. Just like you, I believe that I need to take some time to get used to my full form again. This change is drastic and unexpected."

"This is going to be strange," Menzuo said.

"It will, but I know we will be okay," Solar responded.

Krystal shook her head, still in complete shock. "This is going to take some time to digest. Spaceships on the moon, flying people in the sky, floating faces in my living room, and now issues within Hero City that our child has to face. It's just too much, way too quick," she sat back on the couch and closed her eye for a second. "I think I need something stronger than coffee."

Jammal stood and looked to Jeffery and Michael. "After things settle down, I'm going to need to take some time to gather my thoughts. If things change, I may need the both of you to take care of some things for me. We may need to come up with a plan of action to make things happen."

Jeffery and Michael nodded. "I think we can come up with something," Michael responded. "We just need a quick brainstorming session.

"All of this?" Krystal said as she opened her eyes, "I'm still trying to figure out what all of this is."

"You'll have a lot of time to understand it, Krystal," Marianne said with a smile.

"I guess it is time for me to return to my castle," Naos spoke. "Since the threat from Excervo is gone, I must call for mother Earth's return. The last time that I saw her, she was not doing too well."

"Please, send our regards to the mother of this planet," King Eojtaf said.

"I will, and thank you for stepping in like you did, my friend," Ambassador Naos answered. "It takes a great warrior to do what you have done."

King Eojtaf smiled. "Like I said before, what are friends for?"

Naos nodded then turned to Jammal and Solar. "Thank you both for your sacrifice and dedication to the universe. I know that there has been a change for you two, but I have a strong feeling that this will be great for you both."

"I do hope so, Ambassador Naos," Solar answered.

"Thank you both again for risking your lives," Jammal said to Naos and Eojtaf. "I don't know how you knew that we were still alive, but thank you for everything."

"Prince Menzuo, it is my duty as the Ambassador of this planet, to do what I have to, to ensure its safety. I only thank you for returning to a battle that was not in your favor to win. You have proven much to this universe. This is your place to protect," Jammal sat with a smile as Naos continued. He turned to the rest of the people in the room. "Be safe and try not to worry about what is ahead of us. In due time, we will have to deal with our destiny. As Master Kane said, enjoy your time with your family, I know that I will."

"We will, Naos, we promise," Jammal answered.

Ambassador Naos nodded then shouted. "Sensing Densor!" he quickly disappeared from the living room.

"Whoa!" Steven shouted as he jumped back with his eyes wide. "He's gone! How did he do that?"

"Just a little trick that we are taught so that we can move undetected," Jeffery responded.

"Honey, make me one of those stronger drinks when you do," Steven answered.

Master Renzfly stepped forward. "I believe that it is time for all of us to be leaving as well. It has been a pleasure to have met all of you."

Steven stood and shook his hand. "It has been an experience meeting all of you. I really don't know what to say or how to say goodbye."

Master Renzfly smiled. "Then, don't say goodbye. One day when everything is peaceful, I will send a ship to planet Earth to pick all of you up to fly you out to Yardania. There, you will meet the King and Queen of the planet. They are Menzuo's birth parents. Plus, this trip will be great for the Gallo and Tramor family.

Steven looked at Master Renzfly as if he had three heads. "I'm sorry, who are Gallo and Tramor?"

Master Renzfly pointed over to George and Michael Sr. "Those are our real names," George said quickly. "Marianne's name is Nalla, and Stephanie's name is Raina."

Steven's face suddenly turned up. "Oh, you guys have some serious explaining to do."

Everyone chuckled. Master Renzfly spoke calmly. "I believe after all of the madness has settled on planet Earth, all of you will be due for a relaxing vacation.

"Thank you, Master Renzfly," Krystal said with a calm voice. "I can't wait to meet Jammal's, I mean, Menzuo's real parents. I know this is going to be weird, but I think we should know where our son comes from."

Master Renzfly nodded. He turned to the new team. "Solar Warrior's, when Prince Menzuo and Solar are called to Legerdamien, that will be when we begin our training. Relax yourselves and keep your guard up. You never know when the time will come to battle for the protection of this universe.

"We understand, Master Renzfly," Scoop said in return. "We all will make the best of our time with our families."

"Thank you, Scoop," Master Renzfly answered. "When the time comes, we must work hard and be as prepared as possible for Lord Fetid's return. It will not be an easy war, and it may even be your last."

"We understand, Master Renzfly," Princess Amiata said. "I know that we will be ready to take on this task."

"She's right about that," Jeffery added.

"We'll be ready, Master Renzfly. Don't worry about us," Michael said confidently.

"That is good to hear," Master Renzfly stated. He turned to Steven and Krystal. "It is time for all of us to leave. I will see you both one day soon."

King Eojtaf shook both Steven and Krystal's hands. "It is my honor to have met both of you."

King Scoop and Wyler did the same. "Thank you for having us here. Your son is a wonderful young warrior. You should be very proud," Scoop said.

Princess Amiata and Nuncio walked over to them as well. "Please take care, and thank you for your hospitality. I know that we will see you again," Amiata said.

All of the warrior's stood next to Master Renzfly. They were all ready to leave.

Solar stood and looked to Menzuo. "Well, my brother, I think it will be a great treat for me to finally return home. It will be nice to finally see Yardania again."

Jammal nodded with a smile. "It's funny that we won't be together anymore. It seems strange not having you next to me."

Solar put his hand on Jammal's shoulder. "Little brother, I will always be with you. Just because I am no longer in your diamond, it doesn't mean that we're apart. Our bodies are still linked, but now, I'm lucky enough to have a second chance at life. This is a great gift for me. I will return to our home and train with Master Renzfly to get used to this body. Very soon, I will be ready for what is to come."

"I'm very happy for you, Solar," Menzuo said, then sighed heavily. "I guess things in life have to change sometime, don't they."

"Yes, but in this case, only for the better," Solar turned to Jammal's parents. "Mr. and Mrs. Hall, I have watched both of you over the years and helped out in little ways to make things better. You two are the best parents that Menzuo...I mean, Jammal could ever have."

Krystal hugged Solar. "Thank you, and you can call me mom since you are Jammal's older brother. Any brother of Jammal's is a son of ours."

Solar smiled and hugged her back. After a few seconds, he pulled away and walked over to Master Renzfly and the others. He looked at Jammal with a smile. "I will see you soon, brother."

Jammal nodded. "Bye, Solar...for now," he said, smiling back.

Master Renzfly and the others bowed then joined hands. "See you all very soon. Mega Sensing Densor!" he shouted.

They all quickly disappeared.

"Man! I have to learn how to do that," Steven said.

The phone rang at that exact moment. Krystal answered it. "Hello?" After listening to the message, she hung up.

"Who was it, honey?" Steven said curiously.

"It was a recording from your boss. He said that the office will be closed for the next two weeks. He said that, because of the craziness that just happened today, he doesn't feel comfortable having people come into work. They are forcing everyone to take their vacations and that the company will not charge it against everyone's time."

"Wow," Steven said. "I guess this has scared everyone, huh?"

Krystal nodded. "You do need this break, though."

At that moment, Michael Sr. and George's cell phones rang. After a few seconds, they hung up as well.

They both chuckled. "I guess my boss was just as scared," Michael Sr. answered. "My office is closed for two weeks as well."

George shook his head. "Same here, I guess we should just take this time and relax then."

Steven looked at Krystal with a blank stare. "Honey, I don't know what to say. I know that I haven't been drinking so, is this all real?"

Krystal nodded. "I believe it is. I feel the same way. I can't believe it myself, but why fight it."

Steven sat on the couch. "Now you know that we can't tell anyone about this, right? If we did, they would probably lock us up in the crazy house."

"Or follow us around, thinking that we are aliens, invading Earth. Now that everyone has seen that face in the sky. People are going to come up with all types of crazy stories."

Steven sighed. "I know. I don't want to be put in that category, trust me. I don't need that type of attention."

"If you guys have any questions, we are here for you," Marianne said as she tried to comfort her friends.

"Trust me," Stephanie jumped in. "Everything is going to be okay."

Steven and Krystal sighed heavily as they sat on the couch, trying to digest the new information about the universe. Everything was not clear to them at the moment. They were about to enter a new realm of knowledge, whether they wanted to or not.

~Menzuo~

As Master Renzfly and the others headed back to the outer realm, the spaceship was filled with confidence. These courageous warriors all had a sense of desperation deep inside of them as they knew that they only had a short time to train before the next universal war. No one was aware of what Lord Fetid was preparing to do.

The only thing that was known was that these warriors would all have to fight, possibly to the death, to save every living being that depended on them. The young Solar Warriors, now guided by Master Renzfly, had no choice but to be ready to take on any task that would be thrown in front of them.

Earth and the rest of the universe were safe for now, as Jammal, Jeffery, and Michael, were becoming more comfortable as warriors of a powerful universal team. Jammal could tell that it was going to take a very long time for his parents to understand what was going on, but he was happy to let them in on his secret.

~Menzuo~

Back on Legerdamien, Master Kane stood next to King Yenzuo. Happy that Menzuo, Solar, and the Solar Warriors were able to destroy Queen Eaziah and her Pirate Drones. Master Kane knew that when the time was right, his two new pupils would be ready to keep their promise and return to the death world. Menzuo and Solar were unaware of what the first universal protector had in store for them.

What they would experience on the death world, could possibly surpass their wildest imaginations of what a warrior is meant to be. If they succeeded in Legerdamien, they might become what the universe needs. Hopefully, Menzuo, and Solar's preparation under Master Kane, would be the answer to the now most powerful world in the universe, planet Excervo. Only time would tell if the young universal protector and the team of Solar Warriors were up for the challenge.

To be continued!!!

ABOUT THE AUTHOR

Keshawn Dodds was born and raised in Springfield, Massachusetts on February 24, 1978. He still resides there with his wife, Tamara Dodds and daughter, Sydney Sharee Dodds. Becoming known as a well-established football player in Springfield, he was awarded a football scholarship to American International College in 1997. Mr. Dodds played football all four years at A.I.C., and later graduated with a B.S. in Education in 2001 and a Master of Education in 2009.

After graduating with his Bachelor's degree, Keshawn went on to become a fourth and fifth grade elementary school teacher within the Springfield Public Schools. During his tenure, Mr. Dodds taught at the Homer and Washington Elementary Schools from 2001 - 2005. He later took a job under Springfield's Mayor, Charles V. Ryan, as a Mayoral Aide. After his time in the Mayor's office, Keshawn went back to AIC and worked there for ten years and most recently held the position as the Director of Diversity & Community Engagement. Moving forward, Keshawn is now the new Executive Director of the Springfield, MA Boys & Girls Club Family Center.

Along Mr. Dodds' career journey, he has also become a

published author of a juvenile fiction series, which is known as the Menzuo - Solar Warrior's series. Keshawn has written eight books within the series, and has currently republished the first book, "Menzuo: The Calling of the Sun Prince," in August of 2010, through Cosby Media Productions and in October of 2015, it became an Amazon.com Best Selling book. Mr. Dodds is also awaiting the release of the highly anticipated second book, Menzuo: Legend of the Blue Diamond. The rest of the books within the eight book series are due out in the years to come.

Mr. Keshawn Dodds is an avid writer and strong supporter of education. His long term goal is to become a well-known educational advocate and motivational speaker. Keshawn wants to continue to spread his words of faith towards obtaining a great education and achieving all goals that a person has set in their life. Being raised by his mother, Elizabeth Dodd, Keshawn was always instilled with what a good education can bring to a person. Mr. Dodds firmly believes that, when hard work meets dedication, success is born.

Follow Keshawn @

Facebook:
www.facebook.com/keshawn.dodds
Twitter:
@IamKeshawndodds
Website:
www.keshawndodds.com

For more information on the Menzuo~Solar Warriors Series, visit: www.keshawndodds.blogspot.com

OTHER OFFERINGS FROM THE DARK SPORES SERIES

MENZUO: LEGEND OF THE BLUE DIAMOND

(BOOK 1)

BY KESHAWN DODDS

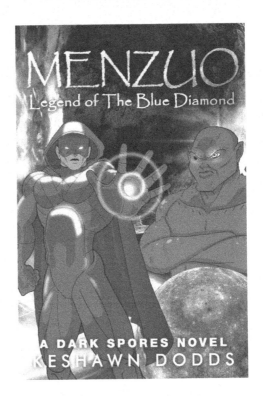

MAJESTIES OF CANAAN:
THE GOLIATH PROJECT

(BOOK 2)

BY CHAYIL CHAMPION

A DARK SPORES NOVEL
CHAYIL CHAMPION

THE CAPE

(BOOK 3)

BY BRAXTON A. COSBY

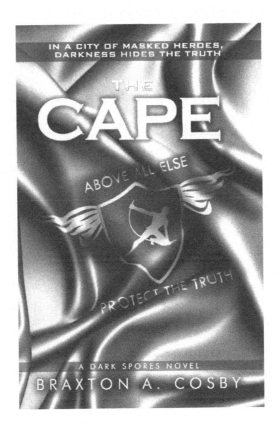

MAJESTIES OF CANAAN:
SECRET OF THE ORAMITE

(BOOK 4)

BY CHAYIL CHAMPION

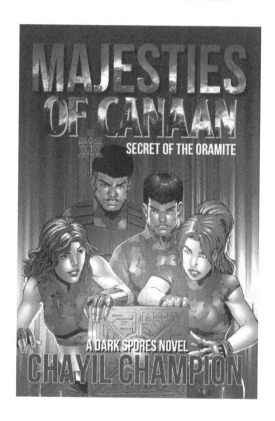

THE CAPE:
OVERDRIVE

(BOOK 5)

BY BRAXTON A. COSBY

REMEMBER TO READ

Menzuo: The Calling of the Sun Prince
Book #1 of the Solar Warriors Series

Menzuo: Legend of The Blue Diamond

CONTINUED IN THE SOLAR WARRIORS SERIES

Menzuo: A Warrior's Destiny

Menzuo: Friend or Foe

Menzuo: Universal War Begins

Menzuo: Lost Archives of Master Kane

Menzuo: Story of Warrior Prince Kenshuo

Cosby Media Productions

Entertaining the Mind, and Inspiring the Soul

www.cosbymediaproductions.com